DOUBLE SHIFTING

MICHAELA GREY

For coyotepup345

1

THE FIRST THING Dima registered was how much his head hurt. It was an all-encompassing ache, starting somewhere on the right side near his temple and radiating out and down. His neck hurt too, his ribs sharply protesting when he took a breath.

The second thing he registered was an insistent beeping. It cut through the fog in his head, drilling right to the center of his brain and making him flinch.

"St-stop," he whispered. He tried to lift a hand but it wouldn't move, something holding it fast. Was he paralyzed? Fear jolted through him and he drew a pain-soaked breath.

"Don't move," a gentle baritone ordered, and the voice was so calming, so familiar somehow that Dima found himself relaxing in spite of the panic still jangling his nerves. "I've called the nurse, just don't move."

Dima tried to open his eyes. The room was dimly lit but even so his retinas felt seared, and he clamped his eyelids shut again, biting back a groan.

The door swung open and crepe-soled shoes squeaked, coming closer.

"I think the beeping is hurting his head," the same voice said, pitched low and soft. "Can it be turned down?"

"Of course," a woman said briskly, and a few seconds later, the beeping receded into background noise. Dima swallowed the grateful lump in his throat, but he was asleep again before he could thank the stranger.

THE NEXT TIME he woke up, his head still hurt but it didn't feel quite as ready to crack open and let his brain spill out. Dima took careful stock. His ribs felt broken—probably at least two of them, he decided. And something was still keeping his hand pinned to the bed. Dima tried to move it, and the weight lifted from it abruptly.

"Hey, you're awake," the same voice said. Dima wanted to know what he looked like, who he *was*, but he was afraid to open his eyes again. "I had them turn the lights as low as possible. It looked like they were hurting your head."

Dima cracked one cautious eyelid. The room was almost completely dark, illuminated by light from the hall and running lights set in the floor along the wall, glowing faintly. Dima opened his other eye and turned to the source of the voice.

It was a man about his age with dark circles under his brown eyes. His five o'clock shadow was almost shockingly dark against pale skin, dark curly hair cut close on the sides and longer on top. Mobile brows were drawn together in worry as he met Dima's gaze, but he tried for a smile.

"Hi," he whispered.

"Wh—" Dima cleared his throat. "Who are you?"

THE NEXT SEVERAL minutes were absolute chaos. The man hit the nurse call button several times and four nurses invaded the room, crowding around the bed and pushing the stranger back to give them room to work. Dima's hand felt cold when the man let go of it, but he submitted to the examinations, answering the questions obediently.

"How many fingers am I holding up?"

"Four. Now three. Five."

"What's your name?"

"Dima Lebedev." He had no idea where that answer came from, but the nurse just nodded.

"What year is it, Dima?"

"2012," Dima said immediately.

"And do you know where you are?"

Dima hesitated. "I thought... Finland, but... you're speaking English. What's going on?"

One of the nurses patted his hand. "The doctor will be in to talk to you soon. Hang tight for me."

Several of the nurses left and the man scooted his chair back to the bed. He didn't try to take Dima's hand again, something which Dima was faintly grateful for. His eyebrows were pinched even closer together.

"You really don't remember me?" he asked softly. There was *something* in his voice but Dima was too exhausted and hurting to parse out what.

"Should I?" he said instead.

The remaining nurse, checking his IV, snorted. "Considering you're married to him, I would hope so, honey."

Dima turned to look at the man, who suddenly couldn't seem to meet his eyes. "We're married?" he asked, disbelieving.

"My name is Rory O'Brien," the man offered. "It's, um. 2020, and we—we play together. For the Boston Otters."

Dima stared at him. "We play in the *NHL?*"

Rory nodded.

"And we're *married?*"

Rory's mouth worked, and he shot a look at the nurse.

"Alright, alright," she said cheerfully. "I'll get out of your hair. Doctor's on his way." She pointed at Rory. "You're going to have to leave at ten, visiting hours will be over."

She disappeared before either of them could protest, and Rory scooted another inch closer.

"Why don't I remember you?" Dima whispered. He felt impossibly small and exhausted, and he wanted—he held out a hand without thinking, and Rory grabbed it immediately.

"I don't know," he said. His thumb rubbed rhythmic patterns on the back of Dima's hand. "Maybe the doctor can explain it."

"Don't leave," Dima said, hating how fragile he sounded, but Rory just squeezed his hand.

"I'm not going anywhere."

The door opened again and a small,

brown-skinned man bustled inside. He was balding, with round glasses set on a snub nose. "Mr. Lebedev," he said, consulting the chart at the end of the bed. "I'm Dr. Daniel Hernandez. How are you feeling?"

"My head hurts and I can't remember the last eight years," Dima said miserably. He was holding Rory's hand so tightly it must have hurt, but Rory was making no complaints.

Dr. Hernandez hummed, flipping a page. "Temporary post-traumatic amnesia is not uncommon, especially considering the severity of the injury you sustained. Mr. O'Brien, keep the shocks to a minimum—immersion in present-day life will not help him remember."

"Temporary," Dima said, grasping at the lifeline. "You mean it'll come back?"

"It should," Dr. Hernandez said. He scribbled something on the paper, then rounded the bed and pulled a small penlight from his pocket. He peered into both Dima's eyes, then listened to his heart and lungs. "You've got a bad concussion, so no electronic screens for the next two weeks. That includes phones, tablets, and television. No reading either. After that, fifteen minutes a day, but if your head starts to hurt again, stop immediately. Someone will need to be with you to observe your symptoms for the first twenty four hours after release, to make sure you're not getting worse."

"I'll do it," Rory said immediately.

Dima said nothing, his head spinning.

"You also have two broken ribs and a sprained wrist," Dr. Hernandez continued. "The wrist needs to be kept immobile for at least a week but it should heal quickly. Your ribs are wrapped. The bandages need to be removed once daily to give your body room to breathe, then reapplied."

"I can't remember all this," Dima said helplessly. His head was aching and he just wanted to go back to sleep.

"I've got it," Rory said, squeezing his hand again, and Dima relaxed. Rory had it. Rory would take care of him. Dima didn't even know who he *was,* but somehow he had absolutely no doubt that Rory would remember every word the doctor said and follow it perfectly.

When the doctor left, Dima looked at Rory, who gazed steadily back. His brown eyes were full of worry, but he managed a smile as Dima stared at him, searching for anything familiar, anything that would trigger a memory.

He liked Rory's face, he decided. Either he hadn't shaved in a few days or he preferred stubble, Dima didn't know, but even several days of growth did nothing to disguise the dimples that flashed when Rory smiled. His nose was long, his mouth wide, and warmth shone from him. Dima wanted to curl up against him, let Rory hold him and keep the world at bay, and he was a little shocked by the impulse. He didn't *know* this man.

Rory's smile slipped and he rubbed his face when Dima said nothing. "I'm—I need coffee. Do you want some?"

"Three creams—"

"Two sugars," Rory finished, standing. His smile was tired. "I know. Be right back."

2

Rory waited until he was safely in the elevator before he pulled out his phone.

"How is he?" Henry demanded.

"He's awake," Rory said, leaning against the wall of the car. "Lucid, talking. In pain, but not complaining, you know how he is."

"When can we come see him?"

"Uh...." Rory didn't know how to even say this. "Look, he—fuck. He has amnesia."

"*What?*"

"He thinks it's 2012. He doesn't remember the last eight years. Not playing in the NHL, not getting traded to the Otters, none of it. He thought he was in Finland."

Henry swore quietly in Swedish.

"There's something else," Rory said.

"What?"

"He, uh." Rory swallowed hard. "When they took him in, I was... upset."

"Yeah, Talkie told me." Henry sounded fond. "Kinda lost your head a bit, didn't you?"

"Beside the point," Rory snapped. "Anyway, um. The nurse asked how I knew Dima, if I was related. Said they couldn't let me back to see him if we *weren't* related, and obviously I can't pass as his brother, so, uh." He took a deep breath. "They think we're married," he said in a rush.

"Oh, *Lorelei*."

Rory suppressed the urge to beat his head against the stainless steel wall. "I know. I *know*. But they wouldn't let me see him, Hank, I was going out of my mind, I didn't know what to do, I just—I didn't really *lie*, but the nurse asked and I didn't... *quite* say no?"

Henry sighed.

"And then a nurse said it *to* Dima, so now *he* thinks we're married but he doesn't remember me and oh my God, this is so fucked up." Rory rolled his head and pressed his cheek to the cold metal wall.

"Does he know what year it is?"

"Yeah," Rory mumbled. The elevator dinged and he straightened and stepped out, heading down the hall to the cafeteria. "But the doctor said to keep him calm, that too many shocks to his system right now aren't good. So I didn't—I haven't told him we're not married."

"Or that you've been in love with him for years," Henry said.

"Definitely not that," Rory agreed, making for the coffee machine. "So when you guys visit, I need you to just...."

"Keep up the pretense," Henry finished.

"Stop finishing my sentences," Rory snapped, then sighed. "Sorry. Yeah. Just... until he's feeling better. I don't want to dump it all on him at once. And maybe his memory will come back on its own and he'll understand why I did it."

"That or he'll punch you for taking advantage," Henry pointed out.

"I'm *not*," Rory protested, filling the second cup. "I'm—I wouldn't, you know that. I'm not going to trick him into bed or anything, come on."

"I know," Henry said gently. "So you want me to tell the team?"

"And Tony?" Rory asked, wincing.

Henry sighed again. "You owe me."

"Babysitting for a year," Rory promised recklessly.

"Oh, you'll regret that, but too late. When can we visit?"

"Doc said tomorrow he can start having visitors, two at a time."

"See you tomorrow," Henry said, and hung up.

Rory shoved the phone in his pocket, gathered up the coffee, and headed back upstairs.

Halfway there, he stopped dead in his tracks at the sight of a man walking toward him. He was short, thinning silver hair cut neatly and curling behind his ears, with a huge silver handlebar mustache.

"Mr. Toscano?" Rory shook himself. "Tony? Did someone call you?"

Tony looked every bit as surprised to see Rory. "Rory? Are you okay? What are you doing here?" His eyes sharpened. "Who's hurt?"

"Dima," Rory said. "Weren't you at the game? You didn't see what happened?"

Tony shook his head. "I—we had to leave early. I've been busy and haven't looked at my phone. What happened to Dima? How bad is it?"

"Jefferson boarded him hard," Rory said, fury welling again at the memory. "He has a concussion and some broken ribs. I'm sure Coach called you."

Tony pulled out his phone and scrolled through his notifications. "Yup, and texted me. Is Dima awake yet?"

"Yes sir. I was just getting him some coffee."

"I'm sure he doesn't want visitors right now, so just tell him I send my best wishes," Tony said.

"Sir," Rory said as Tony turned away. "I, uh… I know it's taking advantage, but I wonder if you could have a word with the head nurse so I can stay with Dima after visiting hours are over? I don't—" He swallowed hard. "He's having a rough time of it. I don't want to leave him."

Tony examined his face with sharp blue eyes that didn't miss a thing. Rory felt like a bug under a microscope, but finally Tony nodded.

"Leave it to me. Let me know when he's feeling better."

"Thank you, sir," Rory said. "I will."

WHEN HE PUSHED the door open to Dima's room and stepped inside, the relief on Dima's face was stark, quickly masked by a clearing of his throat.

Rory held out his coffee and Dima took it, murmuring something grateful. He took a sip and sighed, eyes slipping closed.

"I thought hospital coffee was supposed to be bad," he said, taking another sip.

"This is a good hospital," Rory said as he sat back down beside the bed. "Fancy-ass coffee machines, fresh-baked pastries, the works." He watched Dima's face, tracing the line of his jaw, his heavy lidded eyes, the curve of his full mouth. "I saw our general manager outside. He said to tell you he hopes you feel better soon."

Dima nodded, looking blank. "What happened to me?" he said, cradling his coffee in both hands.

Rory grimaced. "Fucking Dean Jefferson, that's what happened. You were in the corner, digging the puck out. You'd just gotten it away from Smith when Jefferson hit you. You went into the boards at an angle. Hit your head." He took a shaky breath, remembering how the bottom had fallen out of his world. "I thought you were dead," he whispered.

"How long have we been married?" Dima asked abruptly, and Rory nearly dropped his coffee.

"I, uh. Not... long?"

Dima nodded. "How long have we been together?"

Rory breathed deep. "I've been in love with you for the better part of five years," he said, and he knew the raw honesty bled through from the way Dima looked up, gazed at him thoughtfully, lips pursed.

"And how long have I been in love with

you?" Dima asked. "When did we *get* together?"

Rory fumbled for words and was saved by a nurse pushing the door open.

"Time to check your vitals again and for you to nap, Mr. Lebedev," she said cheerfully. "Mr. O'Brien, it seems someone likes you. I've been informed that not only are you to be allowed to stay, but we're moving Mr. Lebedev to a private room soon. It has a pull-out sofa, so you'll be more comfortable there."

Tony. "Thank you," Rory said, swallowing hard. He'd have to find a way to thank Tony as well.

The nurse winked at him and checked Dima's temperature, making reproving noises about it being high, then listened to his chest and took his pulse. Finally she slung her stethoscope back around her neck. "You—" She pointed at Dima. "Sleep. You —" She pointed at Rory. "Not a peep out of you, got it?"

Rory nodded silently, and the nurse swept from the room, flicking the lights off on her way out.

Dima fiddled with the bed, adjusting it until he was lying almost flat. He turned over, grimacing and moving slowly, until he was on his side facing Rory, and stretched one hand out across the mattress.

Rory didn't hesitate. He was reaching out to take Dima's hand before he'd consciously registered the thought, and Dima sighed as if relieved.

"I don't know you," he slurred, his eyelids drooping.

"I'm sorry," Rory said nonsensically.

Dima squeezed his hand. "Rory," he whispered. Pain, exhaustion, and drugs were clearly dragging him down.

"Sleep, sweetheart," Rory murmured, and Dima's mouth curved briefly before his breathing slowed and deepened and his hand went loose in Rory's.

3

THE TEAM DESCENDED on the hospital the next day. The nurse knocked on the door of the small private room they'd been moved to, looking slightly shell-shocked, and beckoned Rory into the hall, where he was set upon by six very large men who all wanted to hug him.

"Guys," he protested, smothered in Jordan's armpit. "Guys, I need to—mmph —*breathe*, Jesus, Army, are you part orangutan?"

"How is he?" Oskari asked when Jordan released him and Rory had managed to put himself somewhat back together.

"Hank told you?"

A chorus of nods.

"Well, he still can't remember anything. And he thinks—"

"He thinks you guys are maaarried!"

Jacob chimed in, pulling a face he probably thought was adorable.

"*No one* is to tell him otherwise," Rory said sharply. "I'll deal with that once I get him home, understand? Does anyone else on the team know?"

"Just the six of us, and the babies only know because they were at Luca's house playing video games when Henry called him," Jonas said.

Oskari, Rory wasn't worried about. Jacob he fixed with a hard look.

"You're not to tell anyone, you get that, right?"

Jacob rolled his eyes. "Yeah man, I get it. I'm not *gonna*. Lebby's my friend too." He looked painfully earnest and sincere, and Rory sighed. The damage was done, in any case.

"Who's first to go see him?"

They sorted it out, Jacob and Oskari going in first as Rory waited in the family room with the others.

"So," Luca said, sitting down beside him.

Rory ignored him. He knew that tone of voice.

Luca scooted his chair closer. "So," he repeated.

"Fuck off," Rory said conversationally,

and Luca grinned, flashing his missing tooth.

"Don't be rude," Jonas said without looking up from his magazine, and Rory sighed.

"Get it over with then."

"How long have you been in love with him, and were you planning on ever telling him?"

"Or us," Jonas added, still apparently absorbed in his reading.

Rory glanced around the room. Henry was watching him, looking equal parts amused and sympathetic, and clearly not going to rescue him. The others just seemed curious.

"It wasn't—isn't—relevant," Rory said.

"Seems pretty fucking relevant to me," Jordan rumbled.

"Yeah?" Rory snapped. "Talk to me about relevant when you've asked that girl out, you know the one you've been pining over for how many years now?"

Jordan shifted his weight. "That's different."

"Is it?" Rory shot back. "Because you're sure fucking gone on her, aren't you? But have you actually *told* her?"

"Rory," Henry said mildly. "I realize you're feeling targeted here, but lashing out isn't nice, and also it won't work, so stop trying to shift the focus."

Rory scowled, crossing his arms. "Sorry, Army," he muttered after a minute.

"S'okay," Jordan said graciously.

Rory looked at the men surrounding him again. Jonas was sprawled in his chair, legs outstretched. He was nose-deep in Country Living but Rory knew he wasn't missing a thing. Beside Rory, Luca had a foot on his knee, hazel eyes intent. Jordan was crammed into the corner next to Henry, his bulk making the chair look toddler-sized.

No one seemed upset. There were no judgmental looks, no discomfort. Jonas had joined the team after Rory had come out, which meant Luca must have told him, or he'd just figured it out on his own. That was just as likely, Rory thought, considering how observant he was.

"Stalling," Henry remarked. He was looking at his phone, so he missed the venomous look Rory flicked at him.

"Don't rush him," Luca said, and Rory blinked at the unexpected support.

"You guys know Dima," he finally said.

"Kinda why we're here," Jordan pointed out.

"No, I mean you *know* him. Like—you know what he's like. You know you can't budge him on something if he's made up his mind."

"Stubborn bastard," Henry remarked, sounding fond.

"No, he just—he's smart," Rory said. "He considers every angle, but he also knows *himself*, right? Like he knows what he wants, what he likes." He could *hear* the way his voice softened, going fond as he thought about how Dima looked when he'd made up his mind, arms folded and mouth a stubborn line. "He's comfortable with who he is."

"Jesus," Luca said. He sounded stunned. "How did I not see it before now?"

"I saw it," Jonas muttered.

So Luca hadn't told him. For some reason, that made Rory's breath come easier. He could trust these men, this core group. These were his teammates, but more than that—they were his friends. He wondered briefly how Dima was doing with Jacob and Oskari.

"He's not interested, and that's okay," he finally said.

Luca lifted a skeptical eyebrow.

"It *is*," Rory insisted. "It... enough. I'm fine, I promise. Look, I—I came to terms with it a long time ago. I date, don't I?"

"Two boyfriends in five years, neither of

which lasted more than three months? Doesn't really count as dating," Henry said.

"I've been busy," Rory said, but it was feeble and he knew it.

He was saved by the door opening and Jacob bounding through, followed by Oskari.

"He doesn't remember a *thing*!" Jacob announced. "At least about us."

"How many lies did you tell him?" Rory asked.

"Seven, I think," Oskari said in his heavy accent. "But I told him truth in Finnish."

"Is that why he was laughing?" Jacob demanded.

Oskari just smiled, looking pleased with himself.

"Us next," Jonas announced, standing.

Luca gave Rory a long look but then followed Jonas from the room. With his main inquisitors gone, no one seemed inclined to pester Rory further. Still, he was fidgeting before Henry and Jordan came back, grinning widely.

"How is he?" Rory asked.

"Tired," Henry said. "Go in there and be with your boy."

Rory was already moving for the door. He hesitated before he opened it. "Guys— thanks. For… coming. Being here."

Jacob waved him off. "Get your ass in there and tenderly mop his brow or whatever it is you guys do when you're alone."

"But no sex in the hospital," Jordan chimed in.

Rory shot them both the finger and slipped through the door.

Dima's eyes were closed, bruised circles beneath them, his head turned toward the window when Rory stepped inside.

"It's just me," Rory said quietly.

Dima opened his eyes and there was no mistaking the relief in them. "Thank God," he said. "They're nice, but—"

"A lot. I know." Rory rounded the bed and sat, hesitating. Would Dima *want* to hold his hand? But Dima was already holding his own out, and relief flooded Rory's system as he took it in both of his. "They love you," he murmured.

"But not as much as you do." It wasn't a question, Dima's eyes steady on Rory's face.

"Pretty sure that's not possible," Rory said, trying for a smile.

"I can't...." Dima's grip tightened. "I can't say it back yet."

"I don't want you to," Rory said immediately. "Not until—unless you mean it."

Dima didn't quite smile, but the lines of tension around his eyes softened. "I remember Henry, though. Or at least I

23

remember playing against him at Worlds. And now we're on the same team?"

Rory smiled at him. "We babysit his boys sometimes. They're still pretty young, but they're already a handful."

"And the team knows—about us." Dima's eyes were drooping but he clearly wanted to talk. "They don't care?"

"They've known about you since you kissed Henry under the mistletoe your first Christmas with us," Rory said dryly, and Dima huffed a small laugh.

"Sounds like something I'd do. And you?"

"I told them my second year, before you got here," Rory said. Dima's hand was warm and solid in his. He suppressed the urge to kiss his fingers. "I wasn't the first, though. There was Carmine. He came out to the team one day. I don't know why, maybe he was just tired of hiding it. But he's so big that no one was going to fuck with him. And I thought—he did it, so can I." The retelling was stark, but Rory vividly remembered the utter terror that had gripped him when he'd stood on blind impulse when Carmine was done talking and blurted *so am I*. How his knees had wanted to dissolve beneath him at the contempt and disgust in some of his teammates' eyes, how Carmine had moved to stand beside him, almost close enough to touch, and asked if anyone had a problem with it. Miraculously, no one had.

Dima's eyes were almost closed and Rory had no idea how much he'd retained. After a minute, though, Dima stirred.

"Who else knows?"

"Um." Rory racked his brain. *Keep the lie as small as possible.* "Just the team, really. Your, um. Parents, and mine, they don't know."

Dima opened his eyes at that, a line forming on his brow. "Why not? My parents know I'm not straight. Surely they'd be fine with it."

"Yeah, but—" Rory shrugged. "We didn't tell my parents and I just thought—it made more sense to wait."

"Speaking of, shit—my parents? Do they know? I mean about—" Dima gestured vaguely at his head.

"Coach called them," Rory said. He stroked Dima's knuckles, feeling the tiny hairs spring back under his finger. "They wanted to fly over but I think Coach convinced them not to. He said they send their love."

Dima relaxed. "I should call them."

"I'll dial the number," Rory said instantly. "You can't look at electronic screens, remember?" He pulled out his phone, dialed, and handed it over. "I'll be in the hall."

"You can stay," Dima protested, but Rory shook his head and slipped from the room.

"MAMA," Dima said when she picked up the phone.

"Mitya, my darling boy," Katina said in Russian, and there was relief and worry and happiness threaded through her voice. "This is what it takes for you to call me?"

"I'm sorry, Mama," Dima said. He closed his eyes and settled back against the pillows. "I didn't want you to worry."

His mother made a *tsk* noise. "I'm a mother, love. It's what I do."

"Mama—I don't... remember."

"Anything?" Katina said sharply.

"Not since 2012. I don't—I play in the NHL? And for the Otters? I live in Boston? I don't—none of this makes sense." Dima ground the heel of his hand against his eye socket.

Katina hummed. "Is Rory there?"

"He—yeah. He was here when I woke up."

"Of course he was. Is he taking care of you?"

Dima hesitated. Did she know? Or was it just a mother's intuition? "He is," he said carefully. "But I don't—I don't remember him."

"You will." Katina sounded full of certainty, and it made something in Dima's soul settle. "Let me talk to him," she continued.

Dima could see Rory's broad shoulders through the window, silhouetted by the light from the hall. Shouting would hurt his head and probably bring angry nurses, so he fumbled for a pencil lying on the table beside him and lobbed it at the glass. Rory turned, and Dima beckoned. He held out the phone and Rory's eyebrows knit but he came into the room and took it.

"Hello?"

Dima leaned back against the pillows and closed his eyes, only half-listening as Rory talked in a quiet voice, explaining what happened.

"Yes ma'am," he finally said. "I'll take him home with me. I promise I'll take good care of him. I'll let you know if anything changes."

When he hung up, he put the phone on the bedside table out of Dima's reach.

"We don't already live together?" Dima asked, eyes still closed.

"You keep a place in the city not far

from me," Rory said. "But you're over...
with me... more often than not."

"Can we go there now?" Dima wanted
suddenly, desperately, to be out of this
sterile hospital room, to be somewhere
comfortable. He wanted to be alone with
Rory instead of having nurses prodding and
prying at him. Tears pricked his eyelids and
he blinked them away.

Rory took his hand. "Soon, Deems," he
said gently. "They have to make sure you're
stable." He hesitated, then cupped the
unbruised side of Dima's face with his free
hand. "Just a little longer, okay?"

Dima turned his face into Rory's palm
and took a steadying breath. *Soon.*

4

THEY RELEASED him from the hospital forty-eight hours later. Rory insisted on him using a wheelchair down to the front entrance, which Dima allowed with bad grace. The car was waiting, and Rory hovered as Dima levered himself into it, grimacing as his ribs protested the movement. Rory slid in the driver's side and then leaned over to buckle him, shoulder brushing Dima's chest. He smelled amazing, an aftershave Dima didn't recognize but that still somehow calmed something deep inside him. He lifted his good hand and touched Rory's face before he could withdraw, and Rory froze.

"Is that—sorry, should I not—"

Rory caught Dima's wrist as he tried to pull away. "Touch me all you want." His eyes were soft as he smiled, but there was something else in his expression, something Dima was too tired to decipher.

Instead he cupped Rory's jaw, ran a thumb across the top of his cheekbone. Rory shivered but didn't move until a car honked behind them.

"Right," Rory said, pulling reluctantly away. "Should probably get us home before we get shanked for holding up traffic."

His driving was careful and steady, no sudden jerks or hard braking to save Dima's head and ribs, and it wasn't too long before they were pulling up outside an apartment building.

"I have a parking space but I'm going to let the valet take it this time," Rory told him as he unbuckled. "I don't want you walking more than you have to."

He got him out of the car, Dima panting with the effort, and gently pulled Dima's arm over his shoulders, snaking an arm around his waist.

"This okay?" he asked.

Dima nodded, breathless from the pain, and allowed Rory to guide them into the building, through a glossy lobby and past an impeccable doorman into an elevator big enough to hold an elephant.

"I'm getting—the impression," Dima managed, "that you—like expensive shit."

Rory laughed, resettling his grip. "I'm a Boston Otter, baby, I can afford it."

"What about retirement?" Dima shot back.

Rory's expression softened.

"What?" Dima asked as the elevator rose.

"Nothing, just—we've had this discussion. Multiple times. You think I spend too much and I should invest more of what I earn."

"Past me was pretty smart," Dima said, and that earned him a grin.

"Present you isn't too shabby either."

The doors slid open and they stepped out into a carpet so thick their feet sank into it. Recessed lighting and running lights along the walls provide a soft glow as they shuffled along the hall slowly until Rory stopped in front of a door and dug out his keys.

"This is me—us."

He pushed the door open and let Dima make his careful way inside, disarming the beeping alarm as Dima looked around.

Nothing looked familiar. Not the enormous leather couch spanning most of the already huge living room, not the artwork hanging on the walls. Not even the small shelf where Rory put his shoes and then waited expectantly as Dima fumbled to get his own off.

Dima swallowed frustration. "I don't— none of this is—"

"Hey, it's okay," Rory said gently, stepping in close so Dima could hold onto him for balance if he needed to. "Doc said it'll probably come back, yeah? Don't try and force it."

Dima swayed into Rory's space and Rory brought his arms up to hold him in an almost automatic motion.

"Easy," he murmured. Dima pressed his forehead into Rory's shoulder and squeezed his eyes shut.

"I'm so tired," he mumbled.

"Well, let's get you into bed," Rory said. He directed him through the apartment, one solicitous hand on Dima's elbow, and into a bedroom flooded with light from the windows bracketing three walls. Rory let go of him and began drawing blinds until the room was dim and Dima could see without wincing. "Hop in, then," Rory said. "Wait—need to pee first?"

Dima shook his head, crawling between the sheets. They were cool and crisp, comforting against his skin, and he couldn't help the moan as he relaxed into the pillows.

Rory moved around the room, picking

up and tidying, but when he was done, he hesitated in the doorway.

"I'm going to make dinner. I'll be just down the hall. If you need me—"

Dima didn't want him to go. Dima wanted him to stay, to crawl into bed with him and bury his nose in Dima's hair. He wanted to fall asleep with Rory's arm around him and his breath steady and warm in his ear.

He nodded. "Thanks."

Rory watched him for a minute and then left.

Dima wriggled around until he was comfortable but it took him a while to fall asleep.

HE WOKE to the smell of frying ground beef. It didn't take him long to use the bathroom and then shuffle in that direction, breathing shallowly to avoid aggravating his ribs.

"Hey!" Rory said. He was standing at the stove, wearing gray sweats and a T-shirt so thin it was almost see-through in places. "Stroganoff okay? How's your head?"

"Hurts," Dima said shortly.

"Hang on." Rory turned to dig through the plastic bag from the pharmacy. "Here."

He held out two pills, which Dima accepted, then hurried to the refrigerator for a drink.

Dima swallowed the pills, washing them down with cold water, and then propped his chin on his good hand to watch Rory cook. His phone rang from the bedroom and Rory looked up.

"I'll get it, don't move." He turned the heat down and jogged for the bedroom, returning with it to his ear. "He's right here," he said, mouthing *sorry* to Dima, who straightened carefully. "It's your sister," Rory said at normal volume. "Can you talk to her?"

Dima groaned. "No."

"I heard that!" Yana said, voice tinny but unmistakable through the phone speaker.

Rory's lips twitched but he waited, eyebrow raised, until Dima nodded.

"Put her on speaker though," he said before Rory handed the phone over. "I have a concussion," Dima added before Yana could protest. "So you'll talk in English because Rory's here and you'll be nice to me. Because concussion."

Yana sniffed. "Glad to see you're still a brat, Mit'ka."

"Because you're such a breath of fresh air, Yanusya," Dima countered.

Rory stifled a snicker, but his face was smooth when Dima glanced up.

"Do *not* call me that," Yana snapped. "How *are* you, though? Mama said it was pretty bad and you have some memory loss. Do you remember me?"

"Unfortunately," Dima said, sighing, and Rory snorted again as Yana huffed.

"You're fine, I can tell," she said. "Rory, not that he deserves it, but please take care of him."

"I will," Rory called from his position at the stove.

"Mitusya, I'll let you go for now, but I expect frequent updates. Bye, Rory, I look forward to actually meeting you in person someday." She hung up before Rory could answer and Dima pushed the phone away.

"Mitusya," he muttered, scowling. "The worst."

"She's fun," Rory said to the sauce he was stirring, and Dima could hear the smile in his voice.

"She's a nightmare," Dima corrected. "Always telling me what to do."

"Well," Rory said mildly, "she *is* your big sister. Comes with the role, or so I'm told."

"No siblings for you?" Dima asked. Rory's back was to him, and if Dima hadn't been watching, he'd have missed the way his shoulders tightened briefly.

"Nope," Rory said. His voice was light. "Guess I was enough hassle, they didn't want to add more."

Dima frowned. "Hassle?"

Rory turned to the cupboards, not looking at him, and didn't answer.

"If we're married, shouldn't I know about your family?" Dima pressed.

Rory took two glasses out of the cupboard and sighed, shoulders dropping. "They're... fine, I guess," he said to the counter.

"Rory," Dima said, and when he looked up, Dima patted the seat beside him.

It took a minute for Rory to move but he finally rounded the counter and sank into the chair beside Dima.

"I don't talk about them much," he said quietly.

Dima waited.

"They didn't have a lot of time for me," Rory said after a minute. "When I discovered hockey, I think they were relieved, because it got me out of the house for long stretches. They asked the parents of one of my teammates to take me to and from practice. I used other kids' hand-me-down equipment for a really long time until they realized I was serious about it, and then it was only valuable if it got me into a good school."

"Did it?"

"Boston College," Rory said, shrugging. "So yeah. But they've never exactly been the warm and loving type. Once I went to college, we basically stopped talking. I don't go home for Christmas, haven't for years."

Dima shook his head.

"It's fine," Rory said almost hastily. "It's not—they didn't abuse me or anything. They were just busy."

"Too busy for their own son?"

Rory lifted a shoulder. "I'd rather not—look, it's not a big deal. Can we talk about something else?"

"I should probably rewrap my ribs," Dima agreed, but before he took his shirt off, he reached out and squeezed Rory's hand. Then he let go and pulled his shirt slowly up and over his head. When he emerged from the fabric, Rory was kneeling in front of him.

"I can do it," Dima protested.

"Does the thought of me helping make you uncomfortable?" Rory asked, and he was already drawing away.

Dima stopped him with a touch. "Nothing about you has made me uncomfortable so far," he said honestly, and he was rewarded with a smile. Dima returned it and lifted his arms so Rory had room to work. His fingers were warm as they brushed

Dima's skin, unwrapping each layer of bandage carefully and piling it on the table. When he was done, he sat back on his heels as if to survey his handiwork, and Dima had to fight the urge to cross his arms over his now-bare chest. *He's seen it all*, he reminded himself.

"When's the next game?" he asked.

Rory rocked fluidly to his feet and returned to the stove. "Day after tomorrow. Home game, though, so at least I won't have to leave you yet."

Horror struck Dima. "You're—you'll have to travel for the away games."

Rory stirred the meat, looking unhappy. "It won't be for long. We'll get a nurse or someone to help, okay?"

"No," Dima said flatly, and startled Rory into looking up. Dima lifted his chin. "It's just wrapping my ribs and wrist, right? I can do that. I don't—I don't want anyone else here."

Rory's eyes softened. "Okay," he said quietly. "If I call you to check in, do you promise not to look at the phone except to answer it?"

"Yeah," Dima said. He couldn't help his smile. "I promise." The pills were beginning to work—he could feel himself getting a little floaty, a little distant. He had an overwhelming desire to hug someone, so he got up and limped into the kitchen.

Rory turned the heat off before facing him. "Hey, what—"

Dima shut him up by wrapping his arms around him. He could feel the startled breath Rory took, and there was a delay of a few seconds before he brought his own arms up and carefully put them around Dima's shoulders.

"Hey, Deems," he whispered.

Dima rubbed his face against Rory's chest. "You smell good."

"Pain meds make you affectionate, got it," Rory said, but he sounded oddly out of breath.

"Tell me about us," Dima said, eyes closed.

Rory took a deep breath and rubbed Dima's shoulders. "You shouldn't be on your feet. Go sit down."

"When did you know you loved me?" Dima asked as he reluctantly obeyed. The chair was comfortable but it meant Rory wasn't touching him, and Dima decided he wasn't a fan.

Rory busied himself assembling ingredients for sauce. He seemed off balance, but when he looked up at Dima, his smile was sweet and genuine.

"You're my center," he said softly. "It

was… I don't know, a few years ago. I passed to you during a game and you scored. I hugged you and your smile…." He took a breath. "I just thought… 'that's it, I wanna be with him forever'." His dimples deepened, and Dima knew somehow that he was about to be self-deprecating. "Took you longer to fall for me, of course."

"Why of course?" Dima asked. "Look at you. Why wasn't I all over you immediately?"

Rory blushed, stirring the sauce a little too aggressively. "I'm not in your head, how would I know?"

Dima made a dissatisfied noise. "So I was an idiot, then."

"*No,*" Rory said immediately. "You're— you had a lot on your mind. The move from Miami, and—"

"I played in Miami?" Dima asked, momentarily diverted.

"Yeah." Rory poured sauce over the noodles and brought a plate to the table. Setting it in front of Dima, he lingered briefly, bending to look into his eyes. "Light's not hurting your head?"

"No." Dima took Rory's hand and pulled gently until Rory got the hint and folded to his knees in front of his chair. Dima looked down at him, searching the lines of his face for any hint of familiarity, and Rory kept his hands in his lap and let him look.

Finally Dima sighed. "Can I—"

"Yes," Rory said immediately.

Dima half-laughed. "You don't know what I was going to say."

Rory lifted a shoulder, lips quirking. "Doesn't matter. Whatever you need, Deems."

"In that case—" Dima cupped Rory's face with his good hand, stroking a thumb over the stubble with gentle sweeps. Then he leaned forward, still holding Rory's eyes. Rory seemed to have been turned to stone. Dima touched his lips to Rory's and felt the sharp intake of breath, but he didn't otherwise move. Emboldened, Dima pressed forward, caressing Rory's lower lip with his tongue.

Kiss me back, he thought, sliding his hand around to the nape of Rory's neck and deepening the kiss. *Please*.

It took another few seconds, but then Rory groaned deep in his throat and went up on his knees, bracing himself on Dima's thighs and kissing him back with a wild desperation.

Dima hummed happily and hung on for the ride. Rory kissed like it was the last thing he'd ever do, arms snaking around Dima's hips to tug him closer.

Which made it all the more confusing when he tore himself away and scrambled to his feet, wiping his mouth with a trembling hand.

"I'm—I can't," he managed, taking a step back.

"Why not?" Dima demanded. His lips felt swollen, bruised, and he touched them with a finger, noting the way Rory's eyes followed the movement. "You were into it, don't try and tell me you weren't."

Rory's throat bobbed. "You're—you don't remember me."

"So? We're *married*, aren't we? Or do you just not want to—"

"I *do*," Rory interrupted, his eyes fierce. "When you remember. When *you* want to kiss me, not because you're trying to trigger a memory or some shit."

Dima scowled, and Rory's face softened. He went to his knees in front of Dima's chair again, gazing up at him.

"I want to kiss you more than anything," he whispered. "But it feels like… it feels like taking advantage of you."

Dima reached out, touched Rory's mouth with his thumb. "I'm beginning to see why I fell in love with you," he murmured.

Somehow, that was the wrong thing to

say. Rory's face shuttered and he pulled away to stand.

"Eat your dinner before it gets cold," he said, turning for the kitchen.

"Did I say something wrong?" Dima asked, bewildered.

The smile Rory gave him was forced. "You couldn't," he said. "I'll be right back."

5

THERE WERE at least thirty missed calls and messages on Rory's phone, most from numbers he didn't recognize. He frowned but didn't bother going through them yet. They probably just wanted to get a statement from him about Dima's injury. He dialed Henry's number.

"Hello, Lorelei," Henry said, sounding tired but patient.

"I have to tell him," Rory blurted, standing barefoot in the hall outside his apartment.

"About that...."

"What?" Rory demanded.

"You haven't checked the news, I take it?"

"Oh, *fuck*." Rory scrambled back inside for his laptop. "*Fuck*! Hank, I'll call you back." Page after page scrolled past, blurring into each other.

RORY O'BRIEN AND DIMA LEBEDEV MARRIED?

HOCKEY SUPERSTARS IN LOVE!

DIMA AND RORY TIE THE KNOT!

RORY AND DIMA—TRUE LOVE?

Rory covered his mouth with a shaking hand as Dima shuffled into the living room.

"What happened?"

Rory shut the laptop, more to protect Dima's head than to hide the websites. "One of the nurses must have gone to the press," he said, sitting down heavily on the futon. "It's, uh… everyone knows."

Dima eased himself onto the couch beside him. "Ah."

Rory buried his face in his hands. How the fuck had it all gone so wrong? "I just wanted to be with you," he said into his palms, voice muffled. "I just—they were taking you away and I couldn't—"

"What are you talking about?" Dima asked gently, nudging his knee.

Rory swallowed hard and dropped his hands. There was nothing for it. If he kept silent any longer, dug the hole any deeper, Dima would never forgive him when his memories came back, and Rory would lose him forever. Still, it was harder than he expected to open his mouth and say, "We're not married."

Silence fell as he died a thousand deaths.

"What," Dima said very quietly.

Rory didn't dare look at him. "The doctor said not too many shocks to your system, that telling you what year it was was bad enough, that I should ease you into—"

"We're not married."

Rory stood up, took a few steps away. "We're, um, not even together?"

"*What.*"

Rory knew that tone of voice. Dima didn't shout, didn't throw things or explode in fury when he got angry. Instead, he got quiet, dangerous like the rime of ice on a lake, freezing cold and ready to drop you into the depths to drown.

Rory didn't know what to *do*, how to make it right. He opened his mouth and Dima lifted a hand. Rory snapped his mouth shut again as Dima got laboriously to his feet, arm around his ribs.

"We're not together," he repeated. "Am I in love with you?"

"No," Rory said, the word choked and short.

"Are you in love with *me*?"

Rory flinched. "I—no." *You're lying to him*, something whispered, and Rory shoved it down and away. *Too much, too soon, and he doesn't love me back.* He dredged up a faint smile. "Except like a brother, of course. You're my best friend."

Dima was looking at him, eyes sharp and intent, flaying Rory open to peer at his soul.

Rory hunched his shoulders under the weight of it. "I'm s-sorry, Deems, I didn't mean to—it just *happened.* The nurses wouldn't let me back to see you, I was losing my mind, I thought you were dying and you didn't have *anyone* with you, and one of the nurses just assumed, and I… I didn't correct her. But then it kept going, and—I didn't know how to stop it."

"How long were you going to let me think we were together?" Dima's voice was still so, so cold, and Rory shivered.

"I was going to tell you," he said. "I wanted you to feel better first. To heal. I thought maybe if your memories came back, I wouldn't *have* to tell you, that you'd just remember and then you'd understand why I said it." He took a step forward, although everything in Dima's bearing warned him not to get too close. "You're my best friend, Deems," he repeated. "We tell each other everything. You'd—you'd have done the same for me, I know you would have. I didn't know you had amnesia at the time, I swear I wasn't trying to take advan—"

Dima held up his hand again. "I need to think."

Rory swallowed the cold lump of misery in his throat and nodded. "I'll... go see Luca and Jonas."

Dima said nothing as Rory gathered his keys and put his shoes on, still standing in the middle of the living room. His slouchy sweater made him look small, fragile somehow, and Rory ached to touch him.

Instead he cleared his throat. "I'll be back before eight. Please... eat something."

Dima didn't even look at him.

Rory dragged in air. "Bye," he managed, and bolted.

AT LEAST DRIVING in Boston traffic demanded enough of Rory's attention that he didn't have time to eat himself alive over the betrayed look on Dima's face, but as soon as he got to Luca's townhouse and turned off the engine, it all came flooding back.

He squeezed his eyes shut, miserable and sick to his stomach. What if Dima couldn't forgive him? What if Rory really had lost him, far sooner than he'd ever expected? He couldn't even bear the thought of life without Dima in it, warm and golden and laughing, the sun Rory circled in helpless orbit.

A knock on the window startled him upright. Luca arched a curious brow.

"Coming inside or waiting for someone to recognize you?"

Rory scrambled out as Luca stepped back. He looked comfortable, sweats and a tank top that bared his arms, hair held back out of his eyes by a fabric headband printed all over with—Rory took a closer look, diverted in spite of himself.

"Daisies?" he asked.

Luca touched his head as if he'd forgotten he was wearing it. "I didn't pick it out."

"Who did?"

Luca turned for the house without answering.

"Where's Jonas?" Rory asked as he followed him inside.

"We don't actually live together," Luca said, giving him a mildly judgmental look. They rounded the corner into the living room and Jonas waved from where he was stretched out on the couch, nose in a book.

Luca cleared his throat. "Drinks."

"Water," Rory called after him, and collapsed on the couch, Jonas pulling his legs out of the way just in time.

"You're more of a mess than usual," he

observed, putting a finger in his book to peer at Rory over the top.

Rory couldn't muster the energy to flip him off. He stared at the ceiling and wondered how he'd ended up where he was. "Cursed," he mumbled.

"You?"

"This timeline," Rory said, and heaved a sigh. "I told Dima. About not being together."

"How'd he take that?" Luca asked, reappearing with three tumblers in his hands. He handed one to Jonas, who took it without looking away from Rory, eyes sharp.

"Oh, he's thrilled," Rory snapped. He cradled his glass, watching the ice shards clink gently together. "He hates me." He sighed again.

Luca sat down in the chair opposite. "He doesn't hate you, don't be so dramatic."

"I pretended we were married," Rory said morosely. "I *lied* to him. I let him k—" He snapped his mouth shut but it was too late.

"You let him what?" Jonas asked, sitting up.

"Absolutely nothing," Rory said, and took a gulp of water.

"Lorelei." Luca's voice was stern.

"Can you not call me that when you're about to yell at me?" Rory whined.

"I'm only going to yell if you're going to be stupid," Luca said.

"So, you're gonna yell," Rory muttered. He set his glass down and crossed his arms. "Get it over with then."

Luca and Jonas glanced at each other and an entire conversation passed silently between them.

"I should have gone to Jake's," Rory mumbled under his breath.

"We're just concerned," Luca said carefully. "This isn't healthy."

"I'm fine," Rory said. "I've handled it for this long, haven't I?" He pulled his phone from his pocket but it was dark and silent. *Dammit.* "Seriously, can we just play some video games and stop dissecting my unhealthy coping mechanisms?"

His phone stayed dark as Jonas rolled off the couch and went to the television in the corner to hunt through the games. Rory resolutely didn't look at it.

ALONE, Dima sat on the couch again. He still couldn't handle being on his feet for long, and he could feel the exhaustion pulling at him with sticky fingers, nausea churning in his gut.

Rory lied to him. Rory let him think they were married. Dima put his face in his hands and groaned. He *kissed* him, he thought, and couldn't help the cringe of embarrassment. He'd thought he was kissing his husband, but—

A pulse of pain spiked through his head and he couldn't help the whimper. It was all too much. He needed to talk to someone but he didn't even know *who*. He didn't know anyone on the team. All his old teammates were in Finland, or playing for different teams, and it wasn't like he could use the phone anyway.

Actually, that wasn't entirely true. He pulled himself upright and limped into the bedroom. Rory had put Dima's phone, keys, and wallet on the nightstand. Dima picked up the phone, carefully not looking at the screen, and held the lock button down.

The phone beeped, indicating it was listening, and Dima said, "Call Henry."

He climbed into the bed as the line rang.

"You shouldn't be on the phone," Henry said in almost-fluent Russian, and Dima closed his eyes at the pure relief of hearing his mother tongue, even if it was slightly mangled.

"I didn't look at the screen," he replied. "I'm—I need to talk to someone."

There was a beat of silence. "Rory told you."

Dima didn't say anything, and Henry sighed.

"I'm on my way."

It took about fifteen minutes before he was knocking on the front door.

Dima dragged himself out of bed and went to answer it. Henry tilted his head, examining him.

"You look like shit, kid," he said cheerfully, and stepped inside.

"Thanks," Dima muttered, and showed him to the living room.

"Where's Rory?" Henry asked as he settled himself in one of the overstuffed chairs.

Dima draped himself carefully across the couch before answering. "Out."

Henry's eyebrows went up. "What happened?"

"He *lied* to me," Dima hissed. His head protested the vehemence of the words, and he winced.

"Did he?" Henry said mildly. "Or did he do exactly what you'd have done if the situation was reversed?"

"How would I know?" Dima shot back.

"I don't remember him. I don't *know* him. *Would* I have done that?"

Henry leaned forward, suddenly sober. "Dima. You would die for him."

Dima glanced away. "I don't know that."

"And you don't know *me,* at least not the me you've played with for the last three years, so it's okay if you don't believe me. But you'll need to trust me on this." Henry sighed. "Maybe he handled it badly, but I think you wouldn't have been any better in his shoes."

"I kissed him," Dima said abruptly.

Henry's eyebrows climbed his forehead again but he said nothing.

"I was trying—I wanted—he's so handsome and he was right *there* and I thought... maybe if I... maybe I'd remember."

"I guess it didn't work?" Henry sounded curious and faintly amused.

"Except where I got kissed within an inch of my life, no. It didn't work," Dima snapped, and Henry laughed out loud.

"You two are so stupid. You're made for each other."

"Hey," Dima protested, nettled.

Henry just laughed again. "I want some tea. No, don't get up, I'll find it. Rory keeps some for you in his pantry. You stay there and rest."

Dima put his head back down on the cushion and thought as he listened to Henry rattling around in the kitchen, humming to himself. If they were as close as Henry said, he couldn't really fault Rory for rolling with the 'married' lie. Of course he hadn't known it would get so out of hand—all he'd wanted was to be there for Dima.

He needed to talk to Rory. He was fumbling for his phone when Henry came back.

"Don't even think about it," Henry warned him, whisking it out of his grasp. He planted himself back in the chair with his tea and scrolled through the notifications with his other hand. "Ah," he said. "Sit up. Try to look less like you're dying."

"I don't want to," Dima whined into the cushion.

"You need to record a video for your fans, they're worried about you."

"Let them worry," Dima muttered, knowing that was grumpy even for him.

Henry snorted. "You don't mean that. Now sit up."

Dima struggled upright and smoothed his hair back, pushing the pain back. When Henry held up the camera and nodded, Dima gave it a wide smile.

"Hey guys," he said in English. "Sorry

for making everyone worry. I'm doing fine, just taking it easy. Go Otters!"

Mercifully, that was all Henry demanded of him. He hit send on the video and put the phone down out of reach.

"I want to call Rory," Dima protested.

"I'll do it," Henry said.

Rory answered on the first ring, asking something in an urgent voice.

"Relax," Henry said. "Your *husband* is fine."

Glaring hurt Dima's head but it was worth the pain. Henry's smile just widened.

"Come home," he said. "He wants to talk to you but I won't let him use the telephone." There was a beeping noise and Henry blinked. "He hung up on me."

Rory was back in record time, tumbling through the front door and into the living room as Henry told a story about his sons that Dima was only half-listening to. Henry saluted him with his mug of tea and Dima pushed himself upright again. Rory looked terrible, his dark eyes haunted and mouth pulled down, shoulders slumped.

Dima patted the cushion beside him. "Come sit."

"That's my cue," Henry said, and stood. He waved off Rory's lackluster effort to walk him to the door, giving Dima a smile as he went by. "Don't fuck it up," he said in Russian.

Dima didn't bother answering. When the door closed behind Henry, Dima patted the cushion again.

"Rory," he said.

Rory took a hesitant step forward, then another, until he was beside the couch and could sink down onto the edge, still poised as if for flight.

Dima sighed. "Stop looking like I'm going to yell at you."

Rory hunched his shoulders, staring at his hands. "I deserve it."

"No, you don't." That got Rory's attention—his eyes snapped up and Dima reached out, took his hand and held it. Rory appeared to be holding his breath, fingers slack in Dima's grasp. "Henry told me how close we are," Dima continued. "That I *would* have done the same for you."

"I'm sorry," Rory said. "You're right to be mad at me."

"I'm not anymore," Dima said, squeezing his fingers. "I shouldn't have been. You were just trying to take care of me. I just—"

"You thought I was taking advantage," Rory whispered. His eyes looked haunted, dark and guilty.

"I thought—" Dima sighed. It was hard

to think. "I'm not sure what I thought. It was like... I thought you were my husband but you weren't—you *aren't*—and I went from thinking you were my partner, this person who knew more about me than anyone else, to...." He groped for the words. "It was like I didn't know *who* you were suddenly. Does that make sense?"

Rory nodded. If possible, he looked even guiltier. "I should have told you," he said, almost inaudible.

"Well, you did," Dima pointed out. Another spike of pain pulsed through his temples and he flinched, swaying.

"You need more medication," Rory said. "Hang on." He was up and gone before Dima could protest, back in minutes with pills and a glass of water. Dima took them gratefully. "You should rest," Rory said. "You're nowhere near well enough to be up so much." He helped Dima to his feet, staying close as Dima made his way to the bedroom.

"I don't think I can sleep," Dima admitted as he slid under the sheet, which Rory pulled up over his shoulders. "I've slept so much, I just—"

"Okay, I have an idea." Rory left the bedroom but he was back almost immediately with an e-reader in his hand.

"I can't read right now," Dima pointed out.

"Which is why I'm going to read *to* you," Rory said. He settled on the other side of the enormous bed and waited expectantly. "Any requests?"

"I can't promise how much I'll be able to concentrate," Dima admitted, rolling over carefully to face him. "But dealer's choice. You pick."

Rory smiled, and Dima was definitely a fan, the way his dimples flashed and his eyes crinkled with amusement.

He was quiet for a few minutes as he—presumably—scrolled through the options available, and something else occurred to Dima.

"I'm sorry," he said.

Rory's eyes widened as he looked up. "You're—why?"

Dima moved one shoulder. "Kissing you. When you didn't—you know."

"Oh." Rory was silent for a minute. A smile flickered across his mouth, there and gone almost in the same instant. "It was a good kiss," he said.

Dima huffed a soft laugh. "Yeah, it was."

Rory smiled at him. Then he cleared his throat, turned his attention back to the book, and began to read.

Dima wanted to keep his eyes open and

watch him, but exhaustion was dragging him down. He didn't recognize the book Rory was reading, so he closed his eyes and let the words wash over and through him.

He was almost asleep when Rory's phone rang in the living room and Rory swore under his breath.

"Sorry," he murmured. "Be right back."

He wasn't right back. Dima listened to his voice, too low to make out the words but the agitation clear in his tone, and after a while, he carefully levered himself out of the bed and made for the living room.

Rory was standing in the middle of the room, eyes closed and free hand pinching the bridge of his nose.

"No," he said, and it sounded like he'd said it multiple times. "*No*, I'm not doing it. I'm not asking *Dima* to do it. Goddammit, how can you even—"

"Ask me to do what?" Dima asked, and Rory's eyes flew open.

"Deems, you don't—go back to bed."

Dima held his ground, lifting his chin. "If this involves me, I have the right to know what *it* is."

Rory groaned. "Tony, I'll call you back. You should sit." This last to Dima, who would have rolled his eyes except that would hurt his head, and besides, his legs *were* a little shaky, so he sat on the couch and waited for Rory to continue.

When he didn't, still standing in the middle of the room, Dima cleared his throat. "Who's Tony?"

"Anthony Toscano. He's our GM," Rory said. He looked wretched, hovering there like he wasn't sure he was welcome, and Dima sighed.

"Sit down already."

Rory obeyed, shifting his weight and still saying nothing.

"And what did he want?" Dima prompted.

"He wants—he saw the newspapers." Rory swallowed hard. "He wanted to know if it was true."

"What did you tell him?"

"That it wasn't," Rory said instantly. "I wouldn't—Deems, I wouldn't—"

Dima touched his knee and Rory went still. "I know. So what did he ask you?"

"He wants us to—" Rory pinched the bridge of his nose again. "He wants us to pretend to stay married until the season is over."

Dima felt his eyebrows climb. "Why?"

"He said it was personal. That it would be a favor to him if we did it."

"Interesting," Dima said thoughtfully.

"What does he get out of us pretending to be married?"

"I don't know, we hadn't gotten that far."

"Huh." Dima considered. "So what's the play?"

"You can't be serious," Rory said.

"I just want to know what he's thinking!" Dima snapped. "I'm not going to say yes *or* no unless I have all the information."

"Okay, yeah." Rory took a breath. "His idea was that we keep up the story, play up the romance of getting married secretly, me letting it slip in the hospital. When we go out, we'd—" He faltered. "We'd have to pretend to be in love. Holding hands. Maybe even kissing."

Dima nodded, unsurprised, and made a gesture for him to continue.

"Why aren't you more freaked out?" Rory demanded. His eyes looked a little wild, and Dima had to stifle the urge to comfort him.

"It's not like we'd *actually* be married," he said gently. "What's Tony's plan again? We 'break up' over the summer?"

Rory nodded, mouth drooping. "He didn't give me a timeline, but he said if we just stay low-key and sort of... drift apart down the road, we could come back in the fall and pick our lives up again. He said it'll help pave the way for more gay players who want to have real relationships while playing, especially if we handle the 'breakup' amicably. We're not the first, but it's still so new—maybe it's just the more positive representation the better." He paused. "I don't know why it matters so much to him. But he sounded—"

"Did he play? Or does he have any kids in the league?"

Rory shook his head. "I think he has a son, but I don't think he ever played. He's only eighteen? Maybe nineteen? And he's—I don't know what it is, but he's sick. Like has his own personal caretaker, that sick. So I doubt he's ever considered going pro, if he can even play. But Tony asked, and he doesn't ask for things from us often."

"Do you like him?" Dima asked.

Rory sighed. "Yeah. I mean, he's focused on the bottom line, because he's the GM, but he doesn't just see us as commodities. He... cares, I guess."

"Well, we have to, don't we?" Dima said firmly.

Rory didn't look at him, plucking at the seam of his pants.

"This is important," Dima said, keeping his voice gentle. "You feel it too, don't you?"

Rory nodded. "I have to—you should lie down again."

"Will you read some more?" Dima countered.

"If you want," Rory said. He didn't sound happy, but he mustered a smile when he met Dima's eyes. He followed Dima into the bedroom and settled on the edge of the bed as Dima got comfortable. "What about your family?" he asked after a minute. "They won't be happy if you actually got married secretly."

Dima opened one eye. "Ah. Good point. I really need to tell them the truth or I risk my sister murdering me for making our mother sad." He rolled his head just enough to look at Rory, who didn't look surprised. "Is that okay?"

"Well, I'd rather you not be murdered," Rory said, but his smile still didn't look quite right. "Of course it's okay, Deems."

"This will be good," Dima said, closing his eyes and pressing his face into the soft pillow.

"Yeah," Rory said, and began to read.

6

Rory waited until Dima was asleep before setting his tablet aside. He took a minute to look his fill at Dima's face, memorizing his features yet again, and then he tiptoed from the room.

He felt almost frantic with suppressed emotion, skin tight and his jaw aching from the way he was clenching his teeth. He needed to burn off energy before he exploded, so he slipped into his running shoes and out the door.

The gym in his building was equipped with state of the art machines, and Rory wasn't quite rich enough to afford his own private workout room, not with the space and flexibility this one gave him. The other residents left him in peace, nodding at him in the hallway but rarely addressing him. Rory liked it that way.

He ran on the treadmill until he was soaked with sweat, pushing away every thought in his head to focus on the burn in his muscles, the sound of his heartbeat in his ears. Nothing mattered, nothing *existed* except for this moment in time.

But it couldn't last. He'd lost track of how long he'd been running before he stumbled and just barely caught himself. His legs were shaking, and he had to make several attempts to stab the power button before he was able to stagger off and away.

A glance at the clock on the wall told him it had been over an hour. Hopefully Dima was still asleep. He dragged himself back up to the apartment and let himself in silently. No sound from the bedroom.

Standing in the kitchen, everything came rushing back. Rory clenched his fists, pressing them to his temples. He couldn't *do* this. He couldn't pretend to be married to Dima. Not when every touch was agony, knowing Dima didn't feel the same way.

Rory bent, resting his forehead against the cool marble of the countertop. What choice did he have, he wondered. People *needed* this, the representation, confirmation that even NHL superstars were gay and could have fulfilling careers.

He groaned aloud. How was he supposed to do it, though? Touching Dima in public, letting the love he felt shine through—that part he could do. Pretending it meant nothing, in private—that was going to be a lot more difficult.

But did he *really* have a choice? He thought back to his fourteen-year-old self, coming to terms with being gay and still determined to play in the NHL. What would it have meant to him if he'd had someone to look up to, someone who could have shown him all his dreams were possible and he didn't have to compromise?

"Fuck," he said. "*Fuck*." He kicked the cabinet and then hopped on his good foot, holding his abused toe. "Ow, ow, mother-fucking *ow*."

He had to do it.

"Rory?" Dima sounded sleepy and confused, and Rory whirled to face him.

"Would you *stop* getting out of bed?" he demanded.

Dima's lips twitched. "You sounded upset. Why are you so sweaty?"

"Sorry," Rory said idiotically. "I went running. I'll go shower." He took a step closer. "How are you feeling?"

"Hungry, bored," Dima said, lifting a shoulder.

"Well, come sit down, I'll reheat the stroganoff," Rory said.

Dima obeyed, wincing. "We never rewrapped my ribs."

"Shit, I need to do that," Rory said. He shoved a plate in the microwave and rounded the counter to scoop up the bandages as Dima skinned the sweater off and lifted his arms. Rory held his breath as he wrapped Dima's ribs in careful swathes. Dima's skin was silken soft under his fingers, dotted with the occasional mole, and Rory wanted to bend forward, press his mouth to the crook of Dima's elbow, *taste* him—

Dima picked up the sweater with a stifled grunt of pain and tugged it on over his head. Rory took a deep breath and stood as the microwave beeped.

"I'll shower while you eat," he said, setting the plate in front of Dima, and escaped down the hall.

When he came back, Dima was only about half-done, and Rory sat down opposite, propping his fist on his chin as Dima shoveled noodles into his mouth.

"It's not your pelmeni," Rory said, amused in spite of himself. "But I guess it'll do."

"'S good," Dima mumbled through his mouthful. "Didn't know you could cook."

"I can't, not that much," Rory admitted. "But your mom gave me the recipe for this a while ago and it was pretty easy."

"So are we doing interviews and stuff?" Dima asked.

Rory grimaced. "Ugh, yeah. Tony has a list, apparently. But they'll come to us, because you shouldn't be going out and doing stuff while you're still injured."

Dima tilted his head and smiled at him, and Rory got briefly distracted by the way his eyes crinkled and his mouth curved. *Focus,* he told himself sternly.

"You don't like interviews?" Dima asked.

"They're boring as fuck," Rory said promptly. "But they're always better with you there."

"Are we still working the amnesia angle?"

Rory considered this. "Maybe not the last eight years thing," he finally said. "But that you're still having trouble remembering some stuff—that'll cover any gaps, I think."

Dima nodded. "Tell me more about... me. Us. The team."

Rory could talk about Dima all day. He brightened. "So the last you remember, you were playing in Finland?"

Dima nodded again. "Thinking about the NHL but not ready to sign."

"Well, you did. Miami drafted you."

"And did I set the hockey world on fire?"

"Not exactly," Rory said, fighting a

smile. "You actually kind of sucked your first year."

Dima's mouth fell open. "I did not."

"Hand to God." Rory kept his face straight with an effort. "You got sent down for most of it."

"I did *not*." Dima looked utterly outraged, and Rory couldn't keep the laughter in any longer.

"You didn't, you're right," he managed through the giggles.

"Oh my god, you *asshole*."

Rory hiccupped with laughter. "You won the Calder your first year."

"Wait, really?"

Rory grinned at him and Dima's lips twitched.

"That sounds more like me. When did I come here?"

"Two years later."

"Have we taken the Cup yet?"

Rory shook his head and Dima deflated slightly. "Not yet," Rory said. "But I think soon."

Dima looked thoughtful.

"Hey," Rory said. "I know you can't look at screens or read, but do you want me to go get your guitar from your place?"

Dima blinked. "I still play?"

"And you're really good. You could make a career out of it if you didn't play hockey."

"No fucking way." Dima clutched his head suddenly, frustration on his face. "God, why can't I *remember*? There's just… so much."

"Hey, it's okay," Rory said gently. "It'll come back. Don't try to force it. How's your head?"

"Still hurts," Dima admitted, and Rory was on his feet immediately, striding for a glass of water and the pills. "You're good to me," Dima said softly as Rory handed him both.

Rory floundered briefly. "It's easy to be good to you," he said lamely, and Dima's lips quirked. He was opening his mouth to say something when his phone rang again, still on the table. Dima reached for it and Rory whisked it away.

"Uh… it's your sister again."

Dima looked blank. "Why—I guess see what she wants?"

Rory answered cautiously. "Hello?"

"Let me talk to him," Yana said.

"Everything okay?" Rory asked despite his better judgment.

Yana took a measured breath. "Rory, I've always liked you. Which is good because apparently you're my *brother-in-law* now—"

Rory froze. His eyes snapped to Dima's. *She knows,* he mouthed.

73

Dima straightened, alarm flashing across his face, but Yana was still talking.

"—If you don't hand the phone to him right now, I swear to God you're next on my list."

Rory shoved the phone at Dima, who flinched.

"I don't want to talk to her," he protested.

"She fucking *scares* me," Rory hissed, covering the speaker with his hand. "And she's *your* sister, so man up and deal with it!"

Dima gave him a filthy look but finally sighed. "Fine. Speaker."

Rory hit the speaker button and put the phone on the table.

"English, Yanka," Dima said. His voice was calm. "And don't shout. I'm guessing you heard the news?"

Rory shifted his feet, looking longingly at the door, but Dima caught his eyes. *Please don't go*, he mouthed, and Rory folded.

Someday, he thought, sinking into the nearest chair. Someday he'd be able to resist Dima's pleading eyes. Today was clearly not that day.

"How could you?" Yana was saying. She wasn't shouting. Her voice was cold and calm, a measure of deadly peace before the hurricane hit, and Rory shivered. "You broke Mama's heart. Are you happy?"

Dima flinched again, misery flashing across his face. "Yana, I can exp—"

"She's *crying*," Yana interrupted. "She won't talk to me. How could you do that to her? Hide something this big? Do you just not love her at all? Embarrassed of your family back in Finland, now you're a bigshot in the NHL?"

"Hey!" Rory snapped before he thought better of it. "That's not fair. Dima loves you guys more than anything in the *world*."

"Really," Yana said flatly.

"We're not married!" Dima said before she could say anything else.

Dead silence.

Dima and Rory looked at each other.

"You're... not married," Yana said, as if she was testing the words.

"No," Dima said quietly, still holding Rory's eyes. "We're not married."

Rory looked away first, down at his hands in his lap.

"But the papers—"

"It was...." Dima sighed. "They took me to the hospital. Rory was with me. Things got... complicated."

"So you didn't get secretly married," Yana said. "You're not actually in love?"

Rory stood before Dima could answer and took the empty plate to the sink. Dima was talking but Rory turned the water on and focused on scrubbing the dish, doing his best not to hear what he was saying.

It didn't take long, but when he turned the water off and looked up, Dima's shoulders were less tense and there was almost a smile on his mouth.

He said something in Russian and Yana laughed. Dima smiled at Rory, inviting him to share his amusement.

There was a rock lodged in Rory's throat. He dredged up an answering smile and raised his eyebrow, asking without words if things were okay.

Dima nodded as Yana continued to talk.

"I'm gonna—" Rory jerked a thumb toward the living room.

"Yana, I'm tired," Dima said instead. "Tell Mama and Papa I love them and I'm sorry. I thought we had more time to tell you, we didn't expect things to happen this quickly."

When he hung up, he pushed himself carefully to his feet.

Rory followed him to the living room. "So they're okay?"

"Yeah," Dima said over his shoulder. He sank onto the couch and leaned back carefully, closing his eyes. "God, why am I so tired?"

"You're healing," Rory said. He didn't look at the long line of Dima's throat.

"When's the first interview?" Dima asked.

It took Rory a minute to collect his thoughts. "Tomorrow, morning of the game, if you're feeling up to it."

Dima nodded. "Might as well get started."

7

THEY SAT side by side on the small loveseat in Rory's living room, their thighs pressed together. Rory was sweating under the lights trained on them but Dima looked cool and collected, no sign of pain or stress in his eyes.

Rory had opened the door to a bevy of people who'd marched into his apartment and set themselves up in his living room as he looked on, feeling helpless. Dima had joined him after a minute, one dark eyebrow going up at the tiny maelstrom in front of them.

It hadn't been much longer before they were ushered to chairs so their makeup could be done and hair fixed. There was no sign of the person set to actually interview them, though. The makeup artist shrugged when Rory asked where she was.

"He'll get here when he's ready."

Now, a harried-looking assistant bustled around them, stopping in her mad dash to lean over and fix Rory's microphone, which had already gotten twisted up. Dima caught Rory's eye and smiled.

"It's just an interview," he murmured, but he took Rory's hand, drawing it into his lap and rubbing his knuckles softly.

"Aw," the assistant said as she straightened. "You guys are adorable."

Dima's smile widened but he said nothing, tightening his grip when Rory tried to pull away.

Rory surrendered to the inevitable as someone knocked on the front door.

"I'll get it," the assistant said. "That'll be him."

Rory listened to the low voices and then the click of heels, and then their host settled opposite them, all flashing white teeth and perfect hair. He introduced himself as Alexander and gave them both a huge smile.

"I don't like to talk before the cameras roll," he said. "I find I get more genuine reactions that way." He made a motion and the red light on the camera nearest Rory flicked on. Rory stiffened in spite of himself, and Dima squeezed his hand again.

"Breathe," he murmured.

"I'm Alexander St. Cloud and I'm here

with Dima Lebedev and Rory O'Brien," Alexander said brightly. "And the news story taking the world by storm—these two love-birds are *married!*"

The camera rolled closer as the operator zoomed in, and Rory forced a smile.

"A little backstory for those who don't know—Rory O'Brien is Boston's own, grad-uating from Boston College before going pro with the NHL. And Dima Lebedev is our star center, born in Russia and then growing up in Finland before making the transition to America to play in the NHL as well. He and Rory have been playing together for nearly six years now." Alexander leaned forward. "Dima, Rory. How did you keep it secret for so long?"

Dima's shrug looked easy, relaxed. "People don't really look too closely if you don't give them a reason to," he said. He was still holding Rory's hand.

"And when exactly did this happen?" Alexander asked.

"Ah well, for that, you'll have to ask Rory," Dima said. He laughed out loud when Rory gave him a filthy look. "Sorry, babe, but you know how my memory is right now."

Rory scowled, but he kept a tight grip on Dima's hand as he focused on Alexander. What had they decided on? "It was at

Christmas," he said. "We spent it together and we just thought… why not?"

Alexander clasped his hands together. "Christmas wedding, how romantic, and that means you're newlyweds! Was your family there?"

"Ah… unfortunately not," Rory said. "We were hoping to have a big party with everyone invited when we were able to come out, but we'd thought that wouldn't happen until at least closer to the end of our careers. In the meantime, we'd planned to host something with family and our closest friends during the summer, but that wasn't exactly how it panned out."

"So how do you think this will affect your playing together?" Alexander asked.

Dima's grip tightened, just briefly, but his voice was even when he responded. "We've been together for two years, Alexander, if anything was going to affect it, I think it would have happened by now." He smiled, and Rory *knew* that smile, inside and out. That was the smile he gave people who'd asked a stupid question. It was patient, and almost pitying, and Rory thought he was the only one who saw the anger lurking beneath. Dima glanced at Rory and arched a brow. "Have *you* noticed any change in our style of play, babe?"

Bantering with Dima, even with pet

names involved, was still the easiest thing in the world for Rory. He grinned at him.

"I'd like you to pass the puck a little more, but we can't have everything."

"Well, I'd like *you* to wash the dishes occasionally," Dima shot back, and his smile was real now, hand warm in Rory's.

Alexander cleared his throat gently and they turned their attention back to him. "What about your team?" he asked. "Any problems there?"

Rory pretended to consider. "Well, Army always leaves his jock on the floor, and Jacob's taste in music is absolutely horrible—"

"Not what I meant," Alexander interrupted, and his teeth showed through his tight smile.

Rory gave him the smile right back, Dima's hand tightening warningly on his. "I know what you meant, Alexander. The team's fine. They all came to see Dima in the hospital. We're a family, and they accept us."

"No one gave you any hassle when you came out?"

"Not that I can recall," Dima said evenly, and Rory bit back the smile. "What about you, Rory? Anyone give you a hard time?"

"Nope," Rory said, just able to resist popping the consonant.

Alexander's eyes narrowed. "What about from other teams? No retaliation?"

"Our relationship was kept to the team only," Rory said. "Jacob tripped me once in practice but I'm pretty sure that was an accident."

Dima laughed softly, but Alexander's smile looked forced.

"So, no concerns of nepotism or playing favorites?"

"Neither of us wear the C," Rory pointed out. "I don't even have an A. Where would the nepotism be happening?"

Alexander shrugged elegantly. "I don't know, it's just a new situation—players on the same team married. I'm sure we're all trying to figure out the dynamics of it."

"There are no dynamics," Dima said quietly. "Rory and I fell in love. We got married. We play hockey together. That's it."

"Well, but surely when one of you has had a bad day, it's hard on the other," Alexander pressed, leaning forward. "What happens if Dima misses a pass, or Rory isn't where he should be? And on the flip side, what if it gives you an unfair advantage on the ice, this sort of bond?"

Rory stared at him. "Marriage doesn't magically bestow telepathy, Alexander."

"Of course not, but the two of you living together, being so close—does it give you more insight into each other's style of play?"

Dima took a measured breath. "Rookies live with veterans all the time. Players room together constantly, become best friends on *and* off the ice. The only difference with Rory and me is that sometimes I kiss him, too."

Alexander looked skeptical. "Does a bad day follow you home?"

"No," Dima said flatly. "Any problems from the rink, from games—all of that is put aside at the door. When we're home it's just us. Besides, it's not like we're the first to come out."

"No," Alexander agreed. "But you're the first to get married."

"So?" Rory couldn't help the sharp tone, and Dima squeezed his hand again. "We're just people, Alexander. We can't stop who we fall in love with, and we shouldn't have to hide it. Dima's been my best friend for a lot longer than he's been my husband. Why wasn't anyone asking us about an unfair advantage before now?"

Alexander opened and closed his mouth. "It's just unprecedented," he finally came up with.

"Really? Because in women's hockey, players marry each other all the time. Or is it only news when men do it?"

"Rory," Dima said quietly.

Rory took a deep breath, throttling back the fury. "I apologize for my tone," he finally said, and even to himself he didn't sound terribly sincere, but Alexander nodded. "Are we about done?" Rory asked.

"Just a few softball questions," Alexander said. "Then we'll let you go. Who hogs the covers?"

"Rory," Dima said immediately.

"Stay in or go out?"

"Stay in," Dima answered again. He was giving Rory time to get himself under control, and Rory was so grateful he could have kissed him. "We're not party people."

"Who's the better cook?"

"Dima for sure," Rory said, proud of himself for sounding calm again, and Dima smiled at him. "Although I don't recommend Russian food on a daily basis as a professional athlete."

"And finally, do you want kids?"

Rory spluttered. "You said *softball*, Jesus!"

Dima snorted a laugh, tightening his grip on Rory's hand.

"We'll edit that out," Alexander told a tech, and gave them another bright smile. "Dima, Rory, it's been a pleasure talking to you both today. Thank you for coming forward and telling your story."

"If we can help even one kid wanting to play and feeling like there's not a place for them, then it's worth it," Dima said honestly.

Rory tried to stand but Dima stopped him with a hand on his arm.

"Let them take the mics off," he said softly, and Rory settled back with poor grace.

They allowed the assistants to untangle and remove the mics, Rory fidgeting as they fussed around them. Dima was calm beside him, unruffled, but Rory felt like he was going to vibrate right out of his skin as Alexander stood, dropped his microphone in his assistant's palm, and left without even looking at them.

"Is he always like that?" Dima asked. He sounded *amused.*

"He was actually on pretty good behavior," the assistant told him. "He hates being on the sports beat. But I'm a big fan."

Dima smiled at her. "What's your name?"

"Alison," she said earnestly.

"I can tell you're good at your job," Dima told her, and Alison's cheeks went pink.

Rory shifted his weight. Why wouldn't the rest of them *leave*? He wanted to punch the wall, vent the towering fury that had built with each pointed question Alexander had tossed at them. Dima took his hand again. He wasn't even looking at him, focused on whatever Alison was saying, but Rory took a slow breath, in and out, and let the contact ground him. *None of it matters,* he reminded himself.

Dima squeezed his hand. "There you are," he said softly.

Rory blinked. The techs were still packing up equipment, and no one was looking at them. He swallowed. "Sorry," he managed.

Dima's eyes creased. "It's okay," he said under his breath.

"Did you hear him?" Rory whispered.

"Making assumptions, implying abuse of privilege, and suggesting that playing together gives us an unfair advantage?" Dima murmured, and his eyes were suddenly hard and cold. "Yeah, I was there." He reached up, hand warm on the back of Rory's neck as he pulled him into a kiss.

Rory's brain blanked out and he let it happen, unable to process anything except the feel of Dima's mouth against his, the fingers rubbing the base of his skull, other hand still wrapped loosely around his wrist. The kiss was soft and close-mouthed, but Rory *wanted*—

He almost made a noise when Dima pulled away.

"Aw," Alison said again, and Rory jerked, recalled to himself. "Sorry," Alison said immediately. "I wasn't—I just wanted to tell you we're ready to head out."

Rory let go of Dima's hand and stood. "I'll walk you to the door."

With them safely on the other side of it, Rory leaned against the wood for a minute to gather his thoughts before heading back to the living room.

"That sucked," he said, and Dima made an affirmative noise. "How are you feeling?" Rory asked.

Dima managed a smile but it was tight with pain. "Need to lie down," he admitted.

Rory helped him up and Dima leaned on him as they made their way to the bedroom.

"They won't all be like that," he said quietly.

"I'll make sure of it," Rory muttered, digging his phone from his pocket. He texted his agent one-handed, but he thought he got his point across, judging from the speed of response. He read it and grunted, somewhat mollified.

"What?" Dima asked as they rounded the corner.

"Matt said he didn't realize it would be

89

that bad and he'll vet the next interviews more thoroughly, make sure they're sympathetic."

"S'good," Dima slurred.

Rory resettled his grip. "Don't fall asleep on me yet. Still gotta get you into bed."

Dima muttered something in Russian and rubbed his face against Rory's shirt. Rory swallowed and eased him into the bed. He handed him his pills, took the water when Dima was done, then pulled the blanket up over his shoulders.

"Tired of this," Dima mumbled, eyes drooping.

Rory physically couldn't stop himself from smoothing his hair back. "I know," he said quietly. "But it'll be better soon."

8

THEY HAD a home game that night. Dima couldn't go, couldn't even watch, and he made his displeasure known as Rory got ready to leave, sitting on the couch with his arms folded and a scowl on his face.

"You're adorable," Rory said without thinking, and slapped a hand over his mouth immediately as Dima's eyes went wide. "Sorry, *sorry*. Inappropriate. Didn't mean to—I—"

"Relax," Dima interrupted. "It's good practice, hearing it. We need to sell this in public, don't we?"

Rory nodded, pulling on his coat and shifting his weight. "You sure you'll be okay?"

Dima patted the small transistor radio Rory had dug out of storage for him. "I'll be fine. I'll listen to everything and you can fill me in on whatever I miss."

Rory wanted to kiss him. He cleared his throat. "See you after," he said, and bolted for the door.

DIMA WAS BORED. He *hated* this, being stuck in the apartment, not being able to even turn on the television to watch the game. He was stuck with this interminable headache and the static from the radio as he waited for the pregame festivities to die down and the announcers to stop babbling about stats and projections.

He stretched out on the couch, grunting as his ribs protested. At least his wrist was better, he thought wryly. One small step at a time.

As comfortably situated as he was going to get, Dima pulled the radio closer and draped an elbow over his eyes to block the light, settling in to listen.

Halfway through, he was ready to throw something, *anything*, if it would keep Rory out of the penalty box. Two for hooking, then another two for tripping, and as if that wasn't enough, he pulled a double minor for fighting.

Dima hurled a cushion as the announcer ran through the laundry list of Rory's sins.

"Of course," the announcer said, his voice dry, "this all could just be pressure that's built up, since as we all know by now, Rory's husband and center, Dima Lebedev, is at home recovering with an upper body injury. Pretty nasty concussion, apparently."

"So you think he's too worried about Lebedev to keep his head on straight?" the other announcer asked, and Dima froze.

"Well," the first said, clearly hedging. "I'm not down there, I can't really say, can I? But it makes you wonder."

"Oh, you son of a bitch," Dima said softly, and turned the radio off just as his phone rang. He winced and answered without looking at the screen. He had a feeling he knew who it was.

"Hello, Dima."

"I'm guessing you're Tony," Dima said.

"I am," Tony said. He sounded amused but also brisk, clearly on a mission.

"I'm also guessing you're calling about Rory."

"Good to see the memory loss hasn't damaged that brain of yours," Tony said. "He needs to get himself under control."

"I know," Dima said. "I'm sorry, I'll talk to him."

"This is important," Tony said. "You're

doing me a favor, and I'm grateful. But this kind of thing—"

"No, I know," Dima said. "Sir—" He hesitated. "Can I ask—"

"You want to know *why* this is so important to me."

"Is it personal?" Dima winced as the words left his mouth. "Sorry. I—you don't have to answer."

Tony said nothing for a minute. Finally he sighed. "This is a conversation that needs to be had face-to-face, I think. Are you free tomorrow?"

"I think so," Dima said. "I'll check with Rory and let you know. And... I'll talk to him. I mean, I've already figured out he's hotheaded. Now I just have to figure out how to talk him down."

"Something tells me you'll figure it out. Just... bear in mind his contract expires next year. Maybe that'll help give you a talking point or two. I'll see you boys tomorrow morning." Tony hung up before Dima could muster a reply.

HE WAS in the bedroom when Rory finally got home, unable to sleep and staring at the ceiling as he fumed, alternately furious with announcers in general and Rory in particular.

Rory knocked softly on the door, a brief rap of knuckles, and put his head in. "Hey, I'm home. How are you doing?"

Dima flicked on the lamp and stared at him for a long minute. Rory looked tired and sheepish, like he knew what he'd done and he was ready for the tongue-lashing. There was a cut on his cheek and a bruise forming, and Dima swung his legs out of bed to stand.

"Let me see," he said, and Rory sat on the edge of the mattress, folding his hands in his lap and tipping his face up.

Dima cupped his chin and inspected the injury. It was a clean hit, clearly, and it would be healed in a few days. He spent another few minutes looking at Rory's face, tracking the mobile eyebrows, the slope of his long nose, the high cheekbones and stark contrast of pale skin against dark hair. He didn't *remember* this man, and he found he badly wanted to, more and more every day.

Rory shifted his weight. "Um."

"Sorry." Dima let go of his chin and stepped back. "I got a call from Tony."

"You shouldn't have answered—"

Dima cut him off. "Not the time to fuss about me. You wanna tell me what you were thinking?"

Rory hunched his shoulders. "Not really."

"Tough," Dima said. "What the *fuck* were you thinking? Do you usually play like that?"

"No!" Rory protested, stung into looking up. "No, I—I mean, I run into goalies sometimes but I don't usually take that many penalties, I swear."

"You shouldn't run into goalies," Dima said automatically. "That's a good way to get jumped."

"It's happened," Rory allowed, lips quirking wryly, and Dima almost smiled back at him. Then he remembered what the announcers and Tony had said.

"They blamed us," he said abruptly, and Rory blinked.

"What? Who?"

"The announcers. Not in so many words, but they implied heavily that because I'm home with an injury, you can't focus or play properly."

"Fuck," Rory muttered, rubbing his scalp.

"This—" Dima gestures broadly to encompass the entire evening. "Can't happen again, Rory. Do you get that? Not if we're doing this for the initiative. Do you really want people pointing at us, using us as an example of a reason to *not* get married because we won't be able to play effectively? That's bad publicity, Rory, and no GM in the world is going to let that happen. Tony as much as said so."

"Well, what's he going to *do*?" Rory shot back, suddenly defiant. "Aren't we helping *him* out here? How exactly is he going to punish us?"

"You're not this obtuse," Dima said.

"Pretend I am," Rory snapped. "Humor me."

"He could *trade us*," Dima hissed. "*You*, specifically, because if we piss him off and you keep playing like you have tonight, where exactly is his incentive to keep you around when your contract expires?"

Rory opened and closed his mouth. "I —shit."

Dima sat down cross-legged beside him. "Now do you get it? If you want to stay, if you want to keep playing in this town— with *me*, Rory—"

"I know," Rory said. "I *know*." He flopped backward onto the bed, arms draped across the mattress. "I'm sorry," he told the ceiling. "I was just—it was stupid."

"Well yeah. Why'd you do it?"

Rory closed his eyes and swallowed. "Couple of players—said some shit. About you. Us, I guess."

Dima had suspected as much, but

hearing it confirmed made his stomach plunge. "What'd they say?" he asked softly.

"Really doesn't matter." Rory opened his eyes and propped himself on his elbows. "I let it get to me. It won't happen again."

His suit was rumpled, the shirt's top buttons undone and tie missing. He still looked unfairly good, and Dima wanted suddenly to peel him out of his clothes, take him apart with his lips and tongue. The impulse startled him and he stood abruptly. "Need to piss," he said, and escaped into the bathroom.

When he came out, Rory was dressed in soft pants and a faded Otters shirt. He was looking in the closet for something, coming up with it triumphantly as Dima stepped into the room.

It was a pillow. "That couch hurts my back," he said. "This'll help."

"Or we could share the bed," Dima said, and Rory's eyes went almost comically wide.

"Deems, you don't—it's okay—"

Dima ignored him and turned to climb back under the covers. He was getting the hang of Rory, he thought. "If we've been friends as long as you say, then it has to have happened at least once."

Rory took a shocked breath. "What does?"

"Us sharing a bed," Dima said. He

squirmed into a position where his ribs weren't complaining, and made an impatient hand flap in Rory's direction. "Come on already, brush your teeth and get in here so you can tell me about it."

Rory stared at him for a long moment but finally he nodded, sharp and jerky, and headed for the bathroom.

When he came back, Dima's eyes were closed but he pulled back the covers. He waited as Rory got comfortable and then turned off the light.

"So tell me," he murmured.

Rory was lying utterly still, several feet away in the ridiculously large bed, but he blew out a breath and turned on his side. "Start of the season, in Denver. The hotel was doing renovations and we had to double up. Ended up in a room with a single king, and you complained to everyone who'd listen the next day that I kicked. I told everyone you snored, of course."

He sounded fond and amused, and Dima hid his satisfaction. He was definitely getting the hang of Rory, he thought. He fell asleep smiling.

9

RORY BELIEVED in being honest with himself, to the best of his ability. So when he woke up to Dima sound asleep with three feet of room between them, Rory was man enough to admit he was disappointed. He lay quietly, watching Dima's face as he slept, and wished he could touch him.

Dima stretched, yawned, and blinked his eyes blearily open. His mouth curved softly when he saw Rory lying beside him.

"You didn't kick," he said, voice graveled with sleep.

"And you didn't snore," Rory said, returning his smile. "How are you feeling?"

"Head hurts," Dima admitted. "But my ribs feel better. What do you have planned today?"

Rory sat up and stretched, yawning. Dima was watching him when he looked back, nothing but friendly curiosity on his face.

"Practice this morning after video review. I imagine I'll get a tongue-lashing from Booth for how I played, too, that'll be fun."

Dima pushed himself upright, grimacing. "You're not—you won't do that again, right?"

"No," Rory said, and twisted to face him. "You were right. It's stupid and reckless and completely opposite what we're trying to do here. Anyway, after practice, we have another interview before the team leaves for the road trip. Are you up to it?"

Dima's grimace turned into an outright scowl but he nodded.

Rory wanted to smooth away the frown, kiss him into smiling again. He cleared his throat and slid out of bed. "Hungry?"

HE MADE scrambled eggs and sausage and toast, burning the edges only a little bit as Dima sat at the table and slowly, carefully skinned out of his shirt so he could unwind the bandages. Rory didn't look at the smooth brown skin that was bared and he didn't offer to help.

Dima muttered something under his breath and prodded his ribs.

"I feel better," he said, looking up.

"You still have to wrap them," Rory said, flipping the sausage, and hid the smile at Dima's glower. "I had no idea you'd be such a pissy patient," he teased.

Dima rolled his eyes. "I'm not *pissy*. There's just no point in this."

"Cough and then tell me that," Rory retorted.

Dima didn't bother to dignify that with a response.

THEY ATE breakfast in companionable silence. Dima didn't seem to notice the burnt toast, eating in quick bites with his unbruised cheek braced on one fist. When they were done, he gathered the bandages and began the laborious process of rewrapping his ribs as Rory cleared the table and set dishes to soak.

It was quiet, homey, and entirely too close to what Rory had dreamed of for years. The only thing that would make it better would be if he could go over to where Dima was sitting, crouch on his heels between Dima's knees and draw him into a kiss.

Now that he knew what Dima tasted

like, how he kissed, the daydreams were even worse. Rory couldn't stop replaying the tiny noises Dima made, the way he sighed against Rory's mouth and rested the palm of his hand on Rory's chest.

Dima cleared his throat and Rory jumped, dropping the dish in his hand. There was amusement in Dima's eyes when Rory looked up.

"Maybe I'm the one who should be looking after you," he suggested.

Rory plunged a hand into the soapy dishwater to find the plate, avoiding his gaze. "Just woolgathering."

"Oh!" Dima said, and Rory dropped the plate again. "Sorry," Dima said, lips twitching. "I forgot to tell you—Tony called last night."

Rory stiffened. "Shit. Is he mad at me? I bet he's mad at me."

"I wouldn't put money on him being thrilled with you," Dima said dryly. "He reminded me that your contract expires this year, so yeah. He's not exactly happy."

"Fuck."

"And he's coming here before practice."

"He's *what*?"

"Sorry, I should have said something sooner. He said he wanted to talk to us face-to-face."

"*Shit.*"

The doorbell rang and Rory shot Dima a panicked look.

Dima reached for his sweater and tugged it laboriously over his head. "Answer it," he said when he emerged from the neck hole.

"But—"

Dima fixed him with a look. "Rory."

Rory growled and spun for the hall.

Tony smiled up at him, blue eyes twinkling. "Thanks for having me."

"Ah… sure," Rory said, and took a step back so Tony could come inside.

Dima met them at the kitchen doorway. "Tony," he said, and held out a hand.

"How are you feeling?" Tony asked, taking it.

"Much better. Would you like something to drink?"

Tony shook his head. "This won't take long."

"Living room," Rory suggested, feeling horribly awkward. He trailed in after them, waiting for Dima to situate himself before sitting down on the cushion beside him as Tony got comfortable in the armchair.

"It's a nice place," Tony said. "Dima, how's the memory?"

"Still mostly gone," Dima said. He sounded much calmer than Rory felt.

"Doctor says it'll come back, we just have to be patient."

"Good, good." Tony leaned forward, eyes suddenly sharp, and Rory gulped. Without looking, Dima reached over and took his hand, still watching Tony, and Tony's mouth curled up. "Rory, you know why I'm here."

Dima's hand was warm, and Rory willed himself to stillness so he wouldn't let go.

"Yes sir," he said when it was clear Tony was waiting for a response.

"Have you ever met my son?" Tony asked.

Rory blinked, thrown. "I—well, I've seen him at games. Met him at the occasional event, I guess? How's he doing?"

"He's dying," Tony said bluntly.

Rory opened and closed his mouth as Dima's hand tightened on his. "I—"

Tony waved a hand. "You don't have to say anything." There was pain in his brusque tone and the set of his jaw, the bitter curve of his mouth.

"No, I do," Rory insisted. "I'm sorry. That's—how old is he?"

"Twenty-two," Tony said, his voice softening. "Acute myelogenous leukemia. Been fighting it for six years. Beat the odds, the scrappy little fucker. Here." He pulled out his phone and unlocked it before thrusting it at Rory.

Dima leaned over to look, shoulder brushing Rory's. "What's his name?" he asked as they looked at a thin young man with huge brown eyes smiling at the camera from a hospital bed, an oxygen tube in his nose and IV line in his arm. There was a hockey stick across his lap, his bony fingers curled possessively around it.

"Diego," Tony said. "Doctors tell us he's stopped responding to chemotherapy. They give him six months, tops."

"Well, if you said he's beaten the odds before—" Rory stopped himself when Tony shook his head.

"There are long term odds and short term. He's—" Tony cleared his throat and held his hand out for the phone. "He won't be coming back from this."

"I'm sorry" seemed horribly inadequate. Rory looked at Dima, who gave him an equally helpless look in response.

"But that brings me to why I'm here," Tony continued. "Diego was going to go pro. Started skating as a toddler, joined a mite league the second he was old enough. He was good, too. His eye for a play—" He shook his head. "He knew where the puck would be and he'd be there before it, every time. Scouts were already watching him, talking to him. But then he got sick, and—"

Dima squeezed Rory's hand again as they waited for Tony to compose himself.

"He was going to be the first out professional hockey player," Tony said.

"Oh," Dima said, comprehension dawning in the single syllable.

Rory glanced at him, confused. "What?"

"Think about it," Dima said gently. "Diego is gay. And he wanted to go pro."

"*Oh*," Rory said.

"He hasn't stopped talking about you two since the news broke," Tony said. "The fact that you're both out, that you're married—well, that he *thinks* you're married—" He swallowed hard. "I've never seen him happier."

"But we're not the first," Rory pointed out. "What about Adam Caron? Or *Saint*?"

Tony's smile was bittersweet. "Adam's on our biggest rival's team. Diego was thrilled to hear the news, but his loyalties run deep. He was even happier to hear about Saint and Carmine, Caz especially, since he used to be ours. But you two—he idolizes you both, especially Dima. His own players, *his* team. Married, proud to be out, to make a difference for people everywhere who think they can't follow their dreams—" He broke off, clearing his throat again. "Sorry," he said after a minute.

"That's why you want us to stay married," Rory said quietly. It made a horrible, morbid sort of sense.

"If you tell the truth, or pretend to get divorced, it would break his heart." Tony's eyes were bright with tears. "That's why I'm asking—I know it's a lot. But if you could—just for a few more months—" His voice wobbled, breath hitching.

"Of course we will," Dima said immediately. "Right, Rory?"

"Of course," Rory echoed. His head was spinning. Dima looked at him. He was still holding Rory's hand. "Of course," Rory said again, louder. "Whatever... whatever you need."

Tony wiped his face furtively. "Thank you," he said, soft and broken.

"Is he well enough for visitors?" Dima asked.

"Not yet. He had a relapse. That's why we were at the hospital when I saw Rory. But in a week or two?"

"Tell us when," Rory said. His eyes burned and shame curdled in his chest. Here he was stressing over his stupid, petty little troubles when people like Diego existed—he wanted to crawl in a hole where no one could see him.

Somehow he kept it together as Tony got up, as he walked him to the door. He even managed a smile when Tony held out his hand for a final shake.

The door closed behind him and Rory leaned against the wall, pressing the heels of his hands into his eyes.

"Fuck," he said softly. When he opened his eyes, Dima was watching him. Rory looked back. "We have to, don't we?" he whispered.

"Yeah," Dima said, just as quietly. He stepped forward and pulled Rory into his arms. "I think we do."

Rory closed his eyes and took a deep breath of Dima's sweet-spicy smell. This was important. He could do this. For Diego.

10

BEFORE HE LEFT FOR PRACTICE, he gave Dima his pills and settled him on the couch with a drink and a small plate of snacks within easy reach before changing his clothes. Dima watched him, one hand tucked under his cheek, when Rory came back in the room and sat to pull on his shoes.

"I'll be back as soon as practice is over," he said.

Dima hummed acknowledgment, eyes drooping. The morning sun struck his hair, turning the tips burnished bronze. "Gonna nap. Don't let Booth bully you and tell Henry I said hi, and thanks." His eyelids slipped closed and Rory tiptoed from the apartment, pulling the door shut with a quiet click.

HE WAS POUNCED on by Jacob when he walked into the dressing room. Rory ducked automatically before Jacob could get an arm around his neck and dodged sideways.

Undeterred, Jacob bounced on his toes and beamed at him. "How is he?"

"Why are you naked?" Rory asked. It was rhetorical—Jacob didn't believe in wearing clothes unless forced to.

Sure enough, he didn't even bother answering except to roll his eyes as Rory stepped around him to head for his stall.

"So?" he persisted, tagging behind him.

"He's fine," Rory said. "He says hi."

"Really?" Jacob asked, clearly delighted.

"Nope," Rory said, and Jacob deflated. Rory didn't bother hiding his smile. "He doesn't remember you, idiot."

"You're not a nice person," Jacob told him, and stomped away, his dramatic flounce ruined somewhat by the fact that he couldn't *go* anywhere without putting clothes on, so he had to settle for flopping in his stall to glare at Rory from across the room.

"Are you bullying the rookies again?" Henry asked.

"He started it," Rory said.

"I can tell you were an only child, if you still think *that* defense works."

Rory scowled as he stripped out of his street clothes and reached for his workout gear.

"How's Dima?" Henry asked.

"He's fine, healing well. He did actually tell me to say hi to you, and thanks."

"Hey!" Jacob yelled.

Rory flipped him off without looking and dragged his shorts on as Henry snickered.

"Glad he's feeling better. And you?"

"I'm fine. I need to talk to you."

Henry's eyebrows went up but he said nothing as Rory pulled a shirt over his head and then gestured for the door.

They ended up in a meeting room down the hall.

"Sure you're okay?" Henry asked.

Rory fidgeted. "Tony came by this morning."

"By your place?"

"He called Dima last night during the game. Dima forgot to tell me until we were having breakfast. He—" Rory rubbed his face and dropped into a nearby chair. "He wants us to keep up the lie for a few months."

Henry's eyebrows were nearly in his hairline. "Why, exactly?"

"Have you ever met his son?" Rory asked instead of answering.

"Diego. Of course, he's a great kid. *Oh.*" Comprehension dawned on Henry's face.

"You're a lot quicker than me," Rory said bitterly. He folded forward and braced his elbows on his knees. "He's dying, Hank."

Henry sat beside him, saying nothing for a few minutes. Finally, he sighed and put a hand on Rory's shoulder. "What are you going to do?"

"What do you *think* I'm going to do?" Rory snapped, straightening. "I'm going to pretend I'm married to the man I'm *actually* in love with. I'm going to give this kid the happy ending he doesn't get to have, because life is shitty and unfair and *awful.*"

Henry rubbed his back silently and Rory tilted sideways until he could rest his head on Henry's broad shoulder.

"Everything about this sucks," he whispered. "And I'm ashamed of myself for even *thinking* that, when Diego—"

"You're allowed to be upset about your life, even if you're not dying," Henry said firmly. "How does Dima feel?"

"He's onboard, of course he is. It's Dima." Rory sighed and sat up. "Thanks for listening. Would you... tell the others? Luca and Jonas and Army?"

"And the rookies," Henry said, nodding. "Of course I will. We have your back."

"Thanks," Rory said. "I should go work out before the trainers come hunting me."

UNFORTUNATELY, more of the team was in the exercise room, and they all wanted to know how Rory had kept his secret for so long.

"*Married*, Lorelei?" Pete demanded, slinging an arm around his neck. Rory wasn't small, but Pete nearly matched Jordan in sheer tonnage. Rory didn't bother trying to get free. "Bad enough you two have been dating without letting us in on it, but *married*."

"You don't need to know everything," Rory said, voice slightly muffled by Pete's armpit. "We only told a few people."

"Ease off," Jordan called from across the room, and Pete—mercifully—let go.

"Tell him to get better and come back soon," Pete told Rory, who nodded. "We're throwing you guys a bachelor party!"

"Oh dear God please don't," Rory said hurriedly.

Pete's face fell. "Oh—"

"I mean," Rory said, thinking fast, "you know we're not really into parties."

"It won't be big," Pete said, and how a two-hundred fifty pound man managed to look like a pleading puppy was beyond Rory. "C'mon, Lorelei, ya gotta let us do *something* for you!"

"It's just—"

Henry put a hand on Rory's shoulder, cutting him off. "I think it's a great idea, Pete." He squeezed warningly when Rory opened his mouth to protest. "We'll host it at my place. And we'll invite Tony and Diego. What do you think, Lorelei?"

Rory shut his mouth with a click. *Shit.* It was a perfect opportunity to show Diego they were in love. "Sure," he said through his teeth, and somehow managed to dredge up a smile.

Pete lit up. "Yo Army, wanna help me plan the party for our boys?"

Rory cut his eyes toward Henry as Pete and Army put their heads together. "I hate you."

Henry's smile was serene. "Love you too."

BOOTH HAD a lot to say about Rory's performance the night before, most of it at full volume. Rory nodded along dutifully, thinking about the picture Dima had made curled up under the blanket from the back of Rory's couch.

Snapping fingers under his nose jolted him back to awareness. Booth was glaring at him.

"Did you hear a word I just said?"

Rory thought back. "Something about self-control and bag skates?"

Booth sighed. "Among other things. Figure your shit out. Now go home to your boyfriend, you're useless to me like this."

"Technically, he's my husband," Rory pointed out, and ducked the pencil Booth hurled at his head on the way out the door.

DIMA WAS STILL ASLEEP when he got home. Rory crouched by the couch, watching his soft breathing, the way his dark lashes lay on his cheeks, his mouth soft with sleep. After a minute he sighed internally and touched Dima's hand.

Dima woke slowly, eyelids fluttering open in stages. His lips curved when he saw Rory. "Hey," he murmured, voice rough with sleep, and touched Rory's face with warm fingers.

"Um. Hey," Rory managed, holding very still. "How was your nap?"

Dima rolled gingerly onto his back and

stretched, arms up over his head. "Was good," he said. "How was practice?"

"Oh, you know." Rory rocked to his feet. "Coach yelled a lot. I scored on Henry a few times—I think he was distracted."

"Nice," Dima said. He pushed himself upright, scowling at the pain, and Rory held out a hand without thinking. Dima accepted it and Rory hauled him gently to his feet.

Standing, they were toe-to-toe. Dima swayed into Rory's body and Rory steadied him with a careful hand on his hip.

"Okay?" he said, only a little breathless.

In reply, Dima put his head down on Rory's shoulder and muttered something in Russian.

Rory closed his eyes. He couldn't resist pressing his cheek to Dima's hair, but after a minute he stepped back, summoning a smile when Dima looked up.

"Lunch," he said, and Dima followed him into the kitchen.

11

THEY WERE DEVELOPING A ROUTINE, Rory thought somewhat despairingly. He made the food while Dima sat at the table and watched, or rested his cheek on one hand. They ate together in comfortable silence, feet knocking together occasionally under the table, and Rory wanted it to be real so badly he thought he'd choke on it.

"When's the next interview?" Dima asked.

Rory checked the time. "They'll be here in an hour. You sure you're feeling up to it?"

Dima hummed and took a bite of salmon. "I'm already bored," he admitted. "Can't read, can't watch TV. There's a song in my head and I can't even write it down."

"I'll go get your guitar after the interview," Rory said. "That way at least you'll be able to play it, and hopefully it'll still be there when you can put it on paper. Oh, also, Pete wants to throw us a party to celebrate our marriage."

"Pete?"

"Teammate. Almost as big as Army. Good guy, although he wouldn't know subtlety if it hit him with a sledgehammer."

Dima snickered. "Did you tell him no?"

"I tried." Rory sighed and then looked up. "How did you know I wouldn't want to do it?"

"I—" Dima frowned. "I don't know. But you don't, do you?"

"I *really* don't, but Henry pointed out that if we invite Diego and Tony, it's a good opportunity to like...." He wasn't sure how to say it.

"Show Diego we're in love?" Dima finished.

"Something like that." Rory speared a carrot stick and crunched through it. "And Henry offered to host."

Dima's lips twitched. "It's a good idea. Fuck, I need to shower."

"Need help?" Rory offered, and then wished the words unsaid as Dima's eyes widened.

"I—no. I think I can manage. But thank you?"

"Sure, yeah. Okay. No problem. I'm gonna just... wash the dishes." Rory stood to clear the table, kicking himself mentally. *'Need help?'* You *need help, you fucking idiot.* He didn't look up as Dima stood and shuffled slowly from the kitchen.

THE NEXT INTERVIEW went much more smoothly. The reporter had clearly been briefed—he stuck to pre-screened questions easily answered, giving them plenty of space and time to craft their replies. Dima laced his fingers with Rory's as the cameras started rolling, and Rory did his best to look like he did it all the time.

He wasn't sure he managed it, stiff and sweaty under the lights, but Dima's smile was soft when he glanced at him, and Rory couldn't help smiling back.

"Can I just say," the reporter—Mark, Rory thought, or maybe Mike—said, "that it's very refreshing to see such wholesome displays of affection between men?"

"Well," Dima said dryly, "isn't that what love looks like?"

"Not always," Mark/Mike said, and he sounded sad. But the next moment he was smiling again, and thanking them for having him, and shaking hands before he helped the techs and his assistant gather their equipment to leave.

Rory made the run to Dima's apartment, thankfully not far away, and came back with his guitar and some things he thought Dima might like to have. Then it was time for him to pack for the road trip. He watched Dima as he shoved clothes in the bag, stretched out on top of Rory's comforter, fingers laced over his stomach.

"You sure you'll be okay without me?" Rory asked, coming out of the bathroom with his toiletries bag.

"I'll be fine," Dima said. "You won't be gone long." He propped himself on one elbow, searching Rory's face. "You'll play smarter, right? Remember why we're doing this."

Rory set the toiletries bag in his duffel. "I will, I promise. As long as you promise to take care of yourself while I can't."

Dima's smile was soft and it made Rory's chest tight. "I'll do my best."

12

RORY WAS a ball of nerves on the airplane, knee bouncing relentlessly as he chewed his nails and wondered how Dima was doing. He reached for his phone to text him half a dozen times before remembering Dima couldn't look at the screen, swearing at himself, and slumping deeper in the seat.

A big hand appeared out of nowhere and shoved down hard on his knee. Rory went still, more out of surprise than anything, as Henry scowled at him from across the aisle.

"Knock it off or you're riding home in the overhead compartment."

"Like to see you try," Rory muttered, but he crossed his arms and tried to set the bulkhead on fire with his mind, holding his knee still with a mighty effort.

Henry sighed. "He's fine. He'll *be* fine."

"He has a concussion and broken ribs and I left him by himself," Rory snapped. "He wouldn't even let me hire someone."

"First of all, he's a grown man," Henry said. "Second, when are you going to tell him how you feel?"

"Precisely never."

Henry didn't take the hint. "How is that fair to either of you?"

"Leave it, Hank," Rory warned.

"I'm just saying," Henry persisted.

"Well, stop," Rory said through his teeth. "Bad enough he has to pretend he's married to me. I'm not putting that on him too." He blew out an explosive breath. "He's had plenty of chances the last five years. There's no *point* in saying something, because then I'll just lose him forever. This —" He gestured vaguely. "It's better than nothing. So just... let go of this fantasy and leave me alone, yeah?"

Henry held up both hands. "I hate to see you doing this to yourself," he said softly, but he settled back in his seat and didn't push the point.

THEY WERE PLAYING THE RAVENS. Not as bad as the Racers, in Rory's opinion, but still not a team he liked. He especially hated their main enforcer, Simon Fall, as mean as he was big. Simon had a gift for getting under his opponents' skins, and he used it relentlessly.

Rory had tangled with him before, but he was determined this time to let it roll off his back. Unfortunately, Simon hadn't gotten the memo.

He winked at Rory, blue eyes sparkling, as they got in position for the faceoff. Rory ignored him, watching Jacob ready himself for the puck drop.

"Too bad Dima's not here," Simon called.

Jacob shot a worried look at Rory, who shook his head. Reassured, Jacob settled back into position, waiting for the referee to drop the puck.

"I mean, if he was here, at least you guys could put up a fight," Simon continued. "Or maybe not, since apparently he's—"

The puck dropped and Jacob knocked it backward between his feet to Rory. Whatever Simon was saying was lost in the ensuing scuffle.

Simon had it out for him, though, and it was clear from the start. He took every opportunity to knock Rory into the boards, tripping him several times and blatantly slew-footing him once. Somehow the officials didn't see, and every time, Rory dragged himself to his feet, teeth gritted, and threw himself back into play.

"Let me handle it," Pete told him when Rory collapsed on the bench after a particularly brutal play, aching in every muscle.

"Don't take a penalty," Rory warned.

Pete patted his knee absently, watching the players on the ice with a gleam in his eye. When it was his turn, he hurled himself over the boards. Rory watched with no small measure of satisfaction as Pete cannonballed into Simon at full speed, knocking Simon off the puck and flinging him backward into the glass.

"Clean hit, clean hit!" someone yelled.

Pete sent the puck into the far end and flashed Rory a grin as he blew past the bench, several Ravens in hot pursuit. Rory grinned back and then winced. He needed a hot bath and a lot of pain medicine, but at least he wasn't the only one, and at least he hadn't lost his temper. Dima would be proud of him.

RORY CALLED him as soon as he got back to the hotel room and turned the television on. There was a college hockey game going, and Rory watched absently as the phone rang through to voicemail three times. He was starting to get worried when it clicked and he heard Dima's voice, slightly breathless.

"I'm here, hey, sorry."

"Are you okay?" Rory demanded.

"I'm fine." There was a rustling noise and Dima grunted softly.

"Deems? What are you doing?"

"Getting into bed," Dima said. "How was the game?"

Rory brushed that off. "It was fine, it was a game. Fall was his usual asshole self, but Oskari's really stepping up. How are you? What took you so long to answer?"

"Are you always this pushy?" Dima asked. He sounded faintly irritated, and Rory took a deep breath, shoving the worry down.

"Sorry. I—sorry. I just want to make sure you're okay."

Dima sighed. "I'm fine. Sorry. I don't like being...."

"Babied?" Rory asked, sitting on the edge of the bed.

"Broken," Dima said. He sounded tired now, and Rory's heart twisted.

"You're not. You'll be better soon."

"Yeah. So seriously, how was the game? Who's Fall?"

"He's a dick." Rory kicked his shoes off and flopped backward onto the bed, staring up at the beige ceiling. "Kept baiting me.

Saying shit about you, tripping me, shit like that."

"Did he hurt you?"

"Just my feelings," Rory said. He was rewarded by a soft snort of laughter and he smiled at the ceiling. "Nah. Nothing a hot bath and some Epsom salts won't fix."

"You did good," Dima said quietly, and Rory felt warm all over at the obvious pride in his voice. "You didn't let him get to you. What about the reporters, did they badger you about me again?"

"No more than usual. They wanted to know how you're doing, how we kept us a secret for so long. The same old stuff."

"Come home," Dima said. He sounded drowsy.

"Tomorrow night. Just a little longer."

Dima didn't answer, and it took a minute for Rory to realize he'd fallen asleep. It was several more minutes of listening to Dima's quiet breathing before he was able to make himself hang up.

13

HE LET himself into the house quietly, doing his best to get his bags in the door without waking Dima. It was late, the second game of the trip going to overtime and then shootouts, and then the plane's departure was delayed for over an hour before they could finally take off. Rory was exhausted, thinking longingly of sleep for at least ten hours, but overriding that was the urge to make sure Dima was okay.

He took his shoes off and padded down the hall in his socks, pulling his tie off as he went. Rounding the corner, he ran face-first into Dima, coming from the bedroom. Dima stumbled and flinched, and Rory caught him on instinct, steadying him.

"Sorry," he said breathlessly. "I didn't—I thought you'd be asleep."

Dima pulled away and knuckled his eyes. "I was. Heard you come in."

Rory took a step closer and looked him up and down. "How are you feeling?"

"Bored," Dima said. His voice was rough with sleep and narcotics, and he swayed into Rory's warmth as if unaware he was doing it, lowering his head to press his face into the crook of Rory's neck. "I don't know you," he mumbled, one hand coming up to grip Rory's T-shirt. "Why... why 'm I so comf'table with you?"

"I guess part of you *does* know me," Rory said, rubbing his back and swallowing back the now-familiar rush of *why can't this be real.* "It's late, let's get you back in bed."

Dima went without much protest, curling up on his side and watching as Rory moved around the room, gathering clothes to sleep in and then ducking into the bathroom to change.

He was almost asleep when Rory came back out, eyes closed and breathing even, and Rory pulled the covers up to his waist, smoothing the fabric before straightening.

"Sleep well," he said quietly.

"Rory—" Dima held out a hand.

Rory didn't argue. He slid under the blankets and squirmed to get comfortable. Dima rolled over, wincing, until they were face-to-face.

"I missed you," he said quietly. "I don't even know your middle name but I hated that you weren't here."

There was a rock in Rory's throat. Breathing was difficult. He traced the slope of Dima's hooded eyes, the wide mouth that smiled so easily. He wanted to kiss him again, roll him onto his back and devour his mouth until Dima was begging for him.

"It's Michael," he finally said, and Dima smiled as his eyes slid shut again.

"Michael," he repeated. "Suits you."

He fell asleep almost immediately but Rory lay awake awhile longer, watching him and wishing for what he couldn't have.

14

DIMA WOKE UP SLOWLY. He was wonderfully pain-free and comfortable, the morning sun kissing his face, covers halfway down the bed. One arm was draped across something solid and warm that rose and fell steadily. Dima lifted his head and looked down into Rory's face. Even in sleep, Rory was turned slightly toward him, as if ready to spring into action should Dima want for anything. His mobile mouth was soft, face relaxed in a way it never was when he was conscious. *Too in his own head*, Dima thought. *Overthinking everything.* There was a strange affection welling within him.

Rory stirred, making a grumbling noise deep in his chest, and squirmed sideways, wedging one leg between Dima's thighs and burrowing his face into his throat with a soft, snuffling sigh.

Dima held very still, keeping his breathing even with an effort. *Why* couldn't he remember this man? What was wrong with him, that he had no memories of a man who clearly knew him inside and out, who just as clearly would move mountains for him? Rory deserved to be known. To be *appreciated.* He ran his fingers down the bumps of his spine, counting the vertebrae, and knew the moment Rory woke up.

He went utterly still but Dima didn't move, curious to see what would happen. After a minute, Rory lifted his head. His eyes were still sleepy but awareness was filling them fast.

"Um," he said. "Sorry." He rolled away and Dima let him go. "How'd you sleep?"

Dima stretched, yawning, as Rory sat up. "Really well. My head doesn't hurt at all."

"Does that mean you're making breakfast?" Rory teased. He stretched, arms raised, and Dima took a minute to appreciate the graceful curve of his spine. Whatever it is they were pretending may not be real, but Dima would have to be dead to not enjoy the eye-candy currently standing, yawning, and ambling into the bathroom, absently scratching his ass as he went.

After a minute, Dima shook himself.

Breakfast. He could do that. He slid out of bed carefully and headed for the kitchen.

By some miracle, Rory had all the ingredients for Dutch babies, and Dima preheated the oven and set to work assembling the batter, humming to himself. The shower shut off and Rory appeared a few minutes later, damp hair curling around his ears.

"I was kidding about breakfast," he protested, sounding guilty.

"Might as well earn my keep," Dima said lightly. He put a hand on Rory's hip and moved him out of the way to retrieve the cast iron skillet from the cupboard. Straightening, he frowned. "How did I know where that was?"

Rory smiled at him, making dimples flash. "Why do you think I keep my pantry stocked? It's not for me—I can barely manage toast. What are you making?"

"Dutch babies," Dima said, setting the skillet on the stove. "Can you start the coffee?"

"I'm assuming we're not having literal children from Holland for breakfast," Rory said, moving to obey.

"You mean I've never made Dutch babies for you before?" Dima asked. He clicked his tongue. "Are you sure we're friends?"

Rory stopped, coffee scoop in hand, and a stricken look flashed across his face.

"I was teasing," Dima said, alarmed. "Rory, don't look like that. What did I say?"

"I'm—" Rory blew out a breath. "It's nothing."

"It's clearly not nothing," Dima said. "Talk to me."

Rory's shoulders slumped. "I… worry. That… maybe we weren't as close as I thought we were. That I—tricked you into this. That if you had your memories back, you'd be—" He swallowed. "You'd be mad at me for… presuming."

"Presuming what, that we're best friends? Rory—" Dima took a step nearer. "There are two explanations for why you fought your way into the hospital to be with me. One is that you're a creepy stalker trying to live out some perverted fantasy." Horror flashed across Rory's face but he said nothing. "The other," Dima continued, putting a hand on Rory's forearm, "is that we really are best friends and you were there for me. How else do you explain how comfortable I am with you?"

"Bad judgment?" Rory attempted a smile.

"Hank said I would die for you," Dima said quietly and the smile slid off Rory's face. "I don't know—I don't *remember* and I hate it so much, but in all of this, everything that's happened, the one thing I've been able to count on is you. I'm willing to trust my gut on this. Rory—" He shook Rory's arm gently. "Stop looking so miserable."

Rory chewed his lip for a minute but finally nodded.

"I want to go out today," Dima said, turning back to the batter. "I'm tired of being inside and it would help, wouldn't it, if we went and had lunch somewhere together? Held hands and acted in love?"

"Yeah," Rory said quietly. "That would help."

"Maybe I'll remember some stuff," Dima said over his shoulder with a smile, but Rory wasn't looking at him, staring down at the coffee maker with a frown.

THEY SPENT THE MORNING QUIETLY. Rory worked out, Dima napped. His head was beginning to ache again but he took a pill when Rory wasn't looking. No way was he missing his chance to get out of the house.

A little before noon, they headed out after Rory fished up a pair of sunglasses for Dima.

"Dual duty," he said, holding them up.

"Hide your face and protect you from the sun." He seemed to have recovered his sweet disposition, his smile loose and easy as he waited for Dima to get his shoes on and then ushered him out the door.

Their destination was a restaurant in the West End. They were recognized when they walked through the gleaming doors, the host ushering them to the back of the room and leaving them with a smile. Several diners seemed to recognize them but no one approached.

"Tell me more about the team," Dima said once they were comfortable.

Rory obeyed. "You know Hank, our starting goalie. He's pretty much the team dad. He's mentioned retirement a few times, so I think it's something he's gearing up for. Oskari's his backup, but he'll be starter soon. He's incredible, lightning in a bottle, and a really sweet kid, too."

"He was at the hospital, wasn't he?"

"Yeah," Rory said. "Him and Jacob, one of our rookies. The ones who visited you in the hospital are the ones who know we're not actually married. Army's a winger, a really good guy. Henry, of course. And then Luca and Jonas, our top d-pairing."

"Are they together?" Dima asked, tilting his head.

"Why do you ask?"

Dima lifted a shoulder. "I don't know, it's just I never hear one's name without the other."

"Truth is, I don't know," Rory admitted. "They're inseparable, but I've never seen or heard them be, like... physically affectionate."

Dima's lips quirked. "Not everyone expresses themselves that way."

"I know," Rory protested, nettled. "But if they *are* together, they've never said anything to us. Or at least not to me."

Dima hummed thoughtfully. "You mentioned someone named Pete?"

"Another d-man," Rory said. "He's the one throwing us the party, and by the way, I managed to talk him out of the stripper in the cake, so you're welcome for that."

Dima laughed, dimples flashing, and Rory grinned back at him.

"And of course Carmine got traded last year. I don't suppose you remember him?"

"Karma," Dima said immediately, but then shook his head. "I—no. Why do I know that name?"

"I mentioned him in the hospital. He's a d-man. Enforcer when it's necessary. He liked people to think he was big and dumb, but he's one of the smartest guys I've played with. He went to the Seabirds." Rory hesitated. "I guess you don't know—"

"I know who the Seabirds are," Dima said, sounding slightly testy. "Did they draft Saint like everyone thought?"

"Yeah, but there's, uh… more to it than that."

Dima raised an eyebrow but the server was coming back for their drink order. Rory waited until she was gone again.

"Carmine, uh… got outed. Maybe six months ago?"

Dima's mouth dropped. "Really?"

"Yeah. And he's dating Saint."

"Holy shit. Holy *shit*. You're telling me *Sinclair Levesque* is gay?"

"So it would seem," Rory said.

"So when you said we weren't the first, you really meant that. Fucking hell, *Saint*. I played against him at Worlds, you know that?"

Rory almost laughed. "Yeah Deems, I know that."

"I always knew he'd be incredible. But I had no idea—"

"No one did. But when Carmine got outed, he came forward. So no, we're not the first. And Saint's been really under the microscope, him and Carmine both, but they're just dating, they're not married."

More people were watching them, some surreptitious, some not, and Dima reached across the table and twined his fingers with

Rory's. Rory stiffened briefly and Dima smiled at him. "Relax," he said softly, stroking his knuckles. "Someone's taking a picture. You said we play on a line together?"

It took Rory a minute to pick up the thread of conversation. "I'm one of your wingers, yes," he finally said. "Army is second-line center, sometimes plays winger for you. And then of course there's Sergei and Ivan and Eero. They're all worried about you. As soon as you're up to it, we should have them over. A few at a time so they don't overwhelm you, of course."

"I'd like that," Dima said, smiling at him. "Has Pete given us a date for this party, and have you invited Tony?"

"Week after next," Rory said. "I haven't... I should do that."

"Text him," Dima suggested.

Rory nodded, fumbling for his phone, and Dima waited to see if he'd pull free. He didn't, unlocking it with one hand and typing with his thumb, and Dima swallowed against what was becoming a familiar sense of want. He was realizing he didn't just like Rory—he was strongly attracted to him, too.

Rory let go as the server appeared with their drinks. Dima let him take a sip but then reached out and recaptured his hand.

Rory coughed, fingers tightening around Dima's, and Dima brought Rory's hand to his mouth and kissed the back of it, keeping eye contact with him.

Rory flushed a dull red all the way to his ears and his mouth opened and closed several times. Dima was *entranced.*

"Tell me how I came here?" he prompted, and it took Rory a few minutes to gather himself.

He rambled about Miami and how Dima came to Boston, but Dima wasn't really listening, focused more on the feel of Rory's hand in his, how his eyes kept flicking down to their hands nestled together on the table, the way he lost his train of thought when Dima thumbed softly across his knuckles.

More and more people were watching, and Dima had his eye on a pair of young women a few tables away who had been talking to each other in hushed, excited tones. Sure enough, they got up and made their way across the room and Dima squeezed Rory's hand in warning as the pair arrived.

Rory tried to pull away and Dima tightened his grip, smiling up at the couple, clinging to each other and clearly trying to figure out how to open the conversation.

"Hi," Dima said helpfully.

The taller girl shoved a hand out and Dima took it.

"I'm sorry to bother you. We j-just wanted to say... thank you," she stuttered. "F-for... you know."

"It means so much," the other girl interjected. "That you're not afraid to be yourselves. That you're *out*. We've been fans for a while, but we didn't *know*—"

Dima stood impulsively and pulled them each into a hug. They sniffled and clung to him and then Rory was there too, holding out a hand for their phones. He took several pictures of them with both phones, then gave them back as they smiled brilliantly at him.

"Can we—" The shorter girl fidgeted. "Could we get a picture of you two? Together?"

"Of course," Dima said immediately. He pulled Rory against him by his belt loop and wrapped an arm around his waist. Both girls *aww'd* in unison and held up their phones. On impulse, Dima turned his head and pressed a kiss to Rory's cheek, making the girls squeal with delight.

Rory was tense beside him but he managed a smile as the girls left and they sat down again.

"You've got to get better at that," Dima commented.

Rory muttered something under his breath.

"You don't like PDA, is that it?" Dima asked.

"PDA is fine," Rory mumbled. His cheeks were pink again. Dima wanted to see how far down the blush went.

He tilted his head. "So it's me?"

"No, it's—" Rory took a drink, obviously stalling. "It's just… what we talked about earlier. I don't want you to feel like I'm taking advantage, or—"

"But you're not," Dima said, reaching for his hand again. Rory didn't flinch this time, folding his fingers around Dima's. "We agreed to do this. I *want* to do this. I can't, though, if you're not onboard."

"I am," Rory protested. "As long as you know it wasn't my idea."

They were interrupted by another couple of fans, and it was several minutes before they were in private again. The server came by the table then and apologized, but Dima smiled at her.

"It's what we signed up for," he said.

"I'll make sure they leave you alone for the rest of your meal," she told him earnestly.

"Don't let me forget to sign something for her," Dima said after she was gone. He studied Rory for a minute. "I think you just need practice."

Rory's eyes widened. "I don't think I like that tone."

Dima smiled at him but Rory didn't look comforted.

"I have an idea," he said, but he refused to elaborate until they were out of the restaurant and walking down the street, hand in hand. They got a few looks, but not very many, and Rory's hand was warm and firm and fit Dima's perfectly.

"So what's the idea?" Rory prompted.

Dima dodged a tourist. "I think we should have sex."

Rory tripped and only Dima's grip on his hand kept him upright. "You think we should *what*?" His voice was high and a little hysterical.

"Well, why not?" Dima smiled at a little boy who'd clearly recognized him, tugging on his father's hand, but he was focused on Rory, who was still sputtering like a water-logged engine. "You're hot, I'm attracted to you, and you need practice in actually seeming like a couple."

Rory let go of his hand and stopped dead in the middle of the sidewalk. He didn't even seem to notice the swearing and rude looks as people parted to get around him, staring at Dima.

"You're attracted to me?" he said.

Dima took his hand again and pulled him out of the flow of foot traffic. "Rory," he said gently. "I'm not blind. *Or* stupid. Of course I'm attracted to you." He hesitated. "But if you're not—I mean, it's okay if—"

Rory bit his lip. "I am," he said almost under his breath, and Dima moved closer, pressing him back against the glass.

"Yeah?" he breathed.

Rory shuddered, hands coming up to grip Dima's waist. "I d-don't... it's not a good idea."

Dima leaned in and kissed the bolt of Rory's jaw, savoring the soft intake of breath. Rory was hidden from onlookers behind his bulk, their own tiny island of calm in the middle of the bustling West End, and Dima kissed his throat.

"God, you're fucking sexy," he growled in Rory's ear, and Rory groaned, hands tightening. Dima could feel the evidence of his interest thickening against his thigh, but he didn't move.

"What if—"

Dima leaned back enough to see Rory's eyes behind the dark glasses. "What if what?" he asked gently.

Rory chewed his lip for a minute and Dima had to fight the urge to kiss him again. "We're team," he finally said. "Even after this… whatever this is, is over, we still have to play together unless one of us gets traded. If it goes wrong—"

"Like what?" Dima took a step back, giving Rory space to breathe. "It's just sex. We're mature adults. I think we can handle some no-strings-attached sex, don't you?"

Rory ran his hands through his hair, leaving it in disheveled curls. It was enough that Dima thought he could get a hand in it and pull. The thought made him take a breath, and whatever Rory saw in his eyes made him shiver.

"This is not the place to have this conversation," Dima said, and Rory nodded wordlessly.

He followed him into the cab Dima flagged down and they rode back to the apartment in silence. Dima watched him as they rolled through the streets. Rory didn't look unhappy, or disgusted by the idea of having sex with him. But he did look conflicted, back to chewing on his lower lip, long fingers drumming on his thigh. He glanced up once and caught Dima's eye, and a faint smile flickered across his face.

Dima relaxed a fraction. There was affection and warmth in that smile, even if he still looked unsure. Dima leaned back against the upholstery, abruptly disgusted with himself. This was clearly not something

Rory wanted wholeheartedly, and here Dima was trying to talk him into it. He opened his mouth to tell him to forget the whole thing, he shouldn't have brought it up, but Rory caught his eye and shook his head.

Right. Back at the apartment. Dima nodded and Rory's eyes softened briefly before he turned away to look out the window.

15

THIS IS A TERRIBLE IDEA, Rory thought as Dima followed him into the elevator and the car rose. *The worst idea in the history of ideas.* And he couldn't stop *thinking* about it. Not now that he knew Dima wanted it too, had maybe been thinking about it as well. Dima wanted him. Dima was *attracted* to him.

You're going to get your heart broken, said a tiny voice in his head.

My heart's already broken, Rory thought. *Because I'll never really have him. Don't I deserve at least* something *out of this? Something to make up for the fact that he'll never actually be mine?*

Dima still hadn't spoken, even though no one was in the car with them. He was just watching Rory with that lazy, somehow

149

predatory interest that made Rory's gut tighten with need and want.

But when they were safely behind the closed door, Dima was the first to speak and he didn't say what Rory expected.

"I'm sorry" was what he did say.

Rory hesitated, hand on the doorknob. "What?"

Dima hunched his shoulders. "It's pretty obvious you're not interested. I pressured you into this and I didn't—I don't—"

Rory took several quick steps toward him, grabbed Dima's sweater, and pulled him into a kiss, careful not to jostle his ribs. Dima gasped against his mouth but kissed him back urgently, wedging a thigh between Rory's legs and gripping his hips hard enough to bruise. Rory ground down against him, shaking with how good it felt, as Dima got a hand between them to cup his erection, thumb stroking over the taut bulge.

"Fuck," Dima managed when he tore away. Rory dropped his forehead to his shoulder, Dima's hand still working him through the fabric. He was going to come in his pants like a teenager and it would be over before it began.

He wasn't sure how he got the willpower to grab Dima's wrist, but Dima stopped instantly.

"Not good?" he asked breathlessly.

Rory swallowed a half-hysterical laugh and leaned in to kiss him. "*Too* good," he managed against his mouth. Relief filled Dima's eyes, and he kissed him again, gentle and slow this time.

"Should we talk?" he asked when he pulled away.

Rory shook his head immediately. "No. I don't—no. No talking. Please, I just—"

Dima cut him off with a kiss. "Bed?" he suggested, and all Rory could do was nod.

IN THE BEDROOM, it was Dima's turn to stop him, when he reached for the hem of his shirt.

"Let me?" he asked.

Rory swallowed hard and dropped his hands. Dima's smile was soft as he stepped in close and tugged the shirt up and over his head. There was something like awe in his eyes when he surveyed Rory's bare chest, and Rory fought the urge to fidget.

"Deems," he said, aware his tone was verging on a whine, and Dima's smile widened.

"I'm appreciating," he told him. He put a hand flat on Rory's chest, running it down over his abdomen.

"Can you at least—" Rory broke off as Dima reached for his pants. He made quick work of the belt and zipper, pushing the slacks down but leaving Rory's boxers in place. "Oh, f-*fuck*," Rory gasped as Dima folded to his knees. "Don't—Dima, your ribs—"

Dima tilted his head to smile up at him. "I'm fine," he said. He leaned forward and breathed over the damp fabric and Rory stifled a noise with his fist. Dima took his time, no sense of urgency as he closed his mouth over the wet patch and sucked, working the suddenly rough fabric against the head of Rory's cock.

It was nothing like Rory had ever imagined, but it was infinitely better than he'd ever expected. Dima's fingers dug into the muscles of his thighs, small pressure-points of pain morphing into pleasure as he took Rory deeper, soaking the fabric until Rory was gasping, hands opening and closing on nothing to keep from grabbing Dima's hair. His skin felt hot, too tight, every nerve on fire and his knees close to buckling.

He got a moment of unwanted respite when Dima sat back on his heels and yanked his own shirt off. He grimaced as he dropped it but shook his head before Rory could speak.

"I'm fine," he repeated, and pulled

Rory's boxers down. His mouth was scorching wet without the barrier of fabric between them, and he worked Rory with as much enthusiasm as skill, finding the spot under the head that made him cry out when Dima flicked his tongue over it.

Rory reached out blindly, trying to keep himself upright, and Dima grabbed his hand, lacing their fingers together. Rory could feel the orgasm building, heat and pressure at the base of his spine, and he clutched Dima's hand desperately.

"Close," he managed, and Dima pulled off, still stroking, as the pressure snapped and Rory came in a hot, wet rush. It landed mostly on Dima's shoulder but there was a smear on his cheek and Rory couldn't look away, even shaking through the aftermath. He reached out unsteadily and wiped it off with his thumb, but Dima turned his head and grabbed Rory's hand. He kept eye contact as he sucked Rory's thumb into his mouth, and Rory swore, undone. His knees finally gave way and he collapsed gracelessly in a heap as Dima laughed, triumph in it.

"*Fuck*," Rory said, staring at the ceiling. "I think you killed me." He rolled his head to see Dima smiling down at him. There was still hunger in his eyes, and guilt swamped Rory. "Sorry," he said, pushing himself to his elbows, but Dima stopped him with a hand on his chest.

"This is good," he said, and undid his pants. He sighed with relief when he pulled himself out, and Rory licked his lips, staring shamelessly. He'd never seen Dima hard before, and he didn't know if he ever would again, so he took in every detail he could, hungry and wanting. Dima's cock was flushed dark red and it was leaking steadily, pre-come pearling at the tip and sliding in fat drops down the shaft.

Dima was looking at him, Rory realized when he lifted his eyes, and there was a moment that stretched between them, crystalline and fragile, until Dima groaned, the noise ripped from his chest, and he hunched as he came, catching most of it in his palm. Rory held his breath, not sure if he was allowed to touch or not, as Dima wiped his hand on his pants and then sagged sideways.

He ended up half-draped over Rory, who was still flat on his back on the carpet, hair tickling Rory's nose and breath hot on his collarbone. Rory took a chance and stroked his silky hair out of his face.

After a minute, Dima laughed, soundless vibrations against Rory's chest.

"What?" Rory asked, lazy and replete, his mind for once blessedly quiet.

"We never actually made it to the bed,"

Dima said, and bit Rory's pec, making him yelp. He was grinning when he lifted his head. "Shower? This time I think I *do* need help."

Rory groaned at the memory but scrambled to his feet to help him up and follow him into the bathroom.

16

Henry took one look at him at practice the next day and threw his hands in the air. "I don't *believe* this," he hissed.

Rory did a quick check to make sure the words *I HAD SEX WITH DIMA* weren't actually printed anywhere on him, then dragged Henry to the corner of the room.

"Don't make a big deal out of it," he said under his breath.

Henry glared at him and Rory could *feel* himself shriveling under the weight of it.

"It was his idea?" he tried.

Henry's glare somehow intensified.

"It doesn't—didn't—mean anything," Rory said, feeling increasingly like an ant under a microscope at high noon. "He just said—look, it's none of your business. But I'm fine. *He's* fine. We're all fine. How are you?" He winced as Henry's glare went from murderous to—even more murderous, he decided, when he couldn't come up with a suitable simile.

"You slept with him," Henry said between his teeth. "And I'm betting, judging by the *guilt* radiating off your face, that you haven't actually told him how you feel."

"Hey," Rory objected, pointing at him. "We agreed that telepathy is cheating."

Henry was not amused. "Rory," he said quietly, and Rory gave up.

He dropped his head. "He—Hank, he's... I just wanted to know—" To his horror, he could feel his throat closing up and tears pricking his eyelids, and he swallowed hard.

Henry swore under his breath in Swedish and pulled Rory into his arms. "You stupid fuck," he said against his hair, and there was affection and despair in his voice.

Rory closed his eyes and pushed at the tears until they receded and he was reasonably sure his voice would be steady.

"I'm fine," he said when he lifted his head.

Henry raised an eyebrow.

"I'll *be* fine," Rory said, and squeezed Henry's shoulder briefly before stepping away.

DIMA WAS on him the minute he got home, shoving him up against the wall and nipping at Rory's jaw, down his throat, breath hot and hands hungry.

"Christ," Rory managed, knees threatening to buckle.

Dima pulled off and grinned at him. "Hi," he said, and kissed him.

"I'd ask—mmphm—if you missed me," Rory said against Dima's mouth, and Dima laughed softly.

"Not my fault you're so hot. C'mon." He took a step away and pulled on Rory's hand. "Think we can make it to the bed this time?"

HE WAS BETTER THAN FINE, Rory told himself after, Dima dozing beside him with one arm draped over Rory's ribs. For the first time, he didn't have to hide the want that burned inside him. He didn't have to pretend, turn away and disguise the hunger deep in his core that ached for Dima's skin under his palms. Maybe he couldn't say it out loud, but that was okay.

Dima shifted, curling closer, and rubbed his nose against Rory's shoulder.

Rory already had so much more than he'd ever expected to get. He'd be a fool to ask for more. And it *was* making it easier to reach for Dima's hand in public, to let the affection and adoration he felt shine through. That was why they were doing it, wasn't it?

Dima rolled away, leaving Rory feeling suddenly cold. He looked at Dima's sleeping face, swamped by the familiar desperate longing. What was wrong with him, that Dima didn't want or need more of him than this? What was missing? Clearly it was something deficient within Rory himself, because Dima wasn't the type to hide his feelings. Rory was lacking something, that indefinable quality that made Dima sit up and take notice.

He could feel the restless itch beneath his skin starting up again, and he rolled silently out of bed. Maybe a few miles on the treadmill would help shut down the voice in his head.

17

THE DAYS WERE COUNTING down to the party. Tony had confirmed he and Diego would be there, and Henry and his wife were handling the details. All Rory and Dima had to do was show up. Dima was looking forward to it, but he could tell Rory was less sanguine. He still stiffened when Dima touched him, like he was doing something wrong by reciprocating, but once the initial awkwardness was out of the way, there was very real hunger in the way Rory reached for him, the soft, wondering way he explored Dima's body like it was a precious gift he was terrified of breaking.

Dima was drunk on the way Rory reacted to him, the noises he made when Dima kissed him, the soft, hitching breaths when Dima had him in his mouth, the way he was always focused on Dima's pleasure, as if making him feel good was what gave *him* the most pleasure.

At home, it felt like Rory was becoming more comfortable with Dima, letting his guard down. But in public, he still froze when Dima tried to touch him, even taking his hand or touching his arm.

It was weird, he thought, lying on the couch with one arm behind his head. It was like Rory was two different people—the person only Dima got to see, tender and affectionate, and the person the rest of the world saw, shy, awkward, and quiet.

Rory was at practice, and Dima was home, as usual. He was *sick* of it, no matter how nice their place was. He needed to get out, to breathe fresh air, to see something other than the living room walls.

He picked up dark glasses and a hat on his way out the door, shrugging into his coat as he strode down the hall to the elevator. It was a bright, crisp day, the sunlight melting the snow that had accumulated the night before, and Dima stopped on the sidewalk to tip his face up to the sun and take several deep breaths, ignoring the twinge of his ribs. His head ached dully, but he ignored that too. Nothing was going to get him back inside the apartment just yet.

He was able to hail a cab without much

difficulty, and gave the driver the name of the practice facility.

Once there, he pushed through the double doors and followed the sound of skates on ice to the rink itself. It was ringed by seats for a few hundred, with maybe fifty fans scattered throughout watching the practice.

Dima stepped into the rink and made his way down the steps to the players' bench, where several players were sitting.

A huge man with impressive muscles saw him first. "Lebby!" he shouted, and heads turned. The man was grinning. "Yo Lorelei, your husband's here!"

Dima looked up just in time to see Rory trip over his skates and go sprawling. That sent a chorus of hoots and jeers up, but Rory didn't even seem to notice, staring at Dima as he scrambled back to his feet. Dima waved awkwardly as the big man beckoned him closer.

"Get down here, c'mon," he said. "You don't remember me, do you?" He was missing an incisor, his mouth set in what seemed to be a permanent grin.

Dima snuck a look at Rory, who was skating toward them. "Sorry," he said to the stranger. "Don't take it personally."

"Pete," the man said, holding out a huge mitt.

Rory arrived just then and hip-checked Pete sharply out of the way before Dima could shake his hand.

"He probably has rabies," he told Dima as Pete complained. "Um, hi. What are you doing here?"

Dima smiled at him, enjoying the blush crawling up Rory's throat. "I needed to get some fresh air. Hi back."

"Don't be shy on our account," someone vaguely familiar chimed in. He had blond hair and friendly green eyes. "Kiss him hello!"

Rory shot the speaker a venomous glare. "Stay the fuck out of it, Army."

Army snickered as Rory turned back to Dima, rubbing his neck. "Sorry," he muttered.

Dima was standing in the players' box, Rory a good three inches taller on his skates, and a mischievous imp took hold. He reached out and hooked a finger in Rory's jersey, tugging him closer. Rory's eyes went wide but he didn't resist when Dima wrapped a hand around the nape of his neck and pulled him down into a soft, chaste kiss.

Cheers went up from the fans watching, and a chorus of stick taps and whistling from the players on the ice.

Rory broke the kiss first, his cheeks

pink, but his smile was genuine. "How's your head?" he asked under the noise.

Dima smiled back at him, flushed with happiness. "It's fine. Headache, but nothing major." He tugged Rory down for another kiss just because he could, setting off another round of applause as Rory huffed laughter against his mouth.

"Okay, okay, there are delicate eyes watching this," Army called.

Rory glanced over his shoulder. "I'm sure Jake's seen worse."

"Who cares about Jake?" Army demanded. "I'm talking about *me*."

Dima laughed and let go of Rory's jersey. "Get back out there and show off for me."

Rory grinned and obeyed as Dima sat down on the players' bench to watch.

He was good, Dima could see that immediately. His footwork was clean and neat, his passes crisp and precise. He seemed to know where his linemates were without ever having to actually look for them, and Dima applauded along with the onlookers as Rory dropped the puck between his skates in a flawless no-look pass to Jacob.

It shouldn't have been a surprise to Dima that Rory's hockey was so fucking sexy. Still, he couldn't take his eyes off him as Rory deftly avoided three attackers, whipped around the net, and tucked it home before Oskari could stop him.

Rory skidded to a stop beside the bench, and whatever he saw in Dima's eyes made the blush Dima liked so much darken his cheekbones. He coughed, ducking his head, and Dima hid a smile. He couldn't *wait* to get him home. But first Rory had to finish practice, and the coach was blowing the whistle, beckoning the players in.

They gathered near the bench and Dima stood to get closer, attention still fixed on Rory's broad shoulders, his back turned to Dima as he listened to Booth.

A strikingly handsome blond man caught Dima's eye and quirked an eyebrow. He seemed vaguely familiar too—maybe he'd visited him in the hospital? The man grinned, flashing a missing tooth. Beside him was a shorter man with a much broader frame, his dark eyes missing nothing. *Luca and Jonas.* The names fell into Dima's head and he blinked. Luca was from Switzerland, Jonas from Germany. Jonas almost never spoke, and Luca tended to talk for both of them.

Coach blew his whistle sharply to signal the end of the meeting. The sound ripped through Dima's head like a baseball bat through cobwebs, sending lancing pain through his temples. He swayed, closing his eyes, and groped for the bench to ease himself onto it.

Dimly, he heard alarmed voices, but he was too busy fighting the wave of dizziness swamping him to look up.

"Move, *move!*" That was definitely Rory. The bench door swung open and warm hands caught Dima's wrists, steadying him. "Dima?" Rory said from a few inches away. "Are you okay?"

Dima opened one eye. The light seared his retina and he clamped it shut again immediately.

"Is it a migraine?" Rory asked.

Dima thought about nodding and decided he'd rather not throw up all over Rory. He licked his lips. "Yeah," he whispered. "Sorry."

"What does he need, Rory?" That sounded like the coach, maybe. Dima didn't try to see. "He can go to the trainers' room, if you want?"

Rory's hands tightened on Dima's wrists. "You want to lie down in the trainers' room until it goes away? I can go get your pills."

"No." Dima shook his head and then clutched at Rory as the world dipped and swayed again. "I want—home. Please."

"Okay," Rory said softly. "Do you think you can wait until I've changed? I'll be as fast as possible."

"I'll stay with him," someone said.

"Go," Dima rasped.

Rory squeezed his wrists briefly and let go. Dima clutched the bench and listened to the sound of skates through the battering waves of pain.

"It's me," Henry said from beside him.

Dima didn't bother to answer. Any movement at all was agony. He bent forward slowly, breathing through his nose, and rested his elbows on his knees, hanging his head.

Henry was close enough Dima could feel the warmth of his body, but he didn't touch him. He didn't say anything, either, but his silent presence was comforting somehow.

Dima kept his eyes shut and listened to the men leaving the ice, the noise of blades against the surface, usually so comforting, now a jagged scrape against his nerves.

Henry shifted his weight. "Sorry," he said, voice soft and pitched over Dima's head to someone behind them. "He's not feeling well. We'll have to do an autograph another time."

It wasn't long before Rory was back, breathless as he thanked Henry and cupped Dima's elbow to help him to his feet.

"Keep your eyes closed," he directed. "Turn—there you go. Step, six inches high."

He guided Dima up the stairs to the exit, hands and voice unwavering as he described their path. Dima didn't try to see where they were going, letting Rory take the lead. Outside, the sun struck his face and he winced, ducking his head.

"Wait," Rory said, and let go of him. He was back before Dima could panic, draping his jacket over Dima's head. "There. Better?"

It was dark under the jacket, warm and smelling faintly like Rory's cologne.

"Better," Dima said.

"Cab's here," Rory said, and guided him into the backseat. He slid in after him and Dima couldn't stop himself from tilting against his frame. Rory put his arm around Dima's shoulders, gently tugging the jacket up so no sunlight could get through. "We'll be home soon," he whispered.

Somehow, Dima kept himself from throwing up on the drive. His consciousness was blurring around the edges by the time Rory got him in the elevator, the pain battering him from all sides until he could barely keep his feet. Rory was holding him up, an arm around his waist, supporting most of his weight as they made their way down the hall.

"It hasn't been this bad in a while," Rory said as he fumbled the door open. "I'm calling your doctor."

Dima didn't have the strength to argue. He let Rory pour him gently into the bed and pull his shoes off before he tugged the blankets up over him.

"I'm getting your pills," he said.

When he came back, he was talking quietly on the phone. Dima struggled to one elbow and took the pills, gulping them dry and collapsing back into the pillows. Rory sat on the edge of the bed, a hand resting absently on Dima's hip.

"Yeah," he said. "He went to practice today. It was pretty noisy."

Silence as he listened.

"But we went out last week. Had lunch. Nothing happened then. Why now?"

More silence. Dima kept his eyes closed and prayed for oblivion. Rory rubbed comforting circles into his hipbone with a thumb.

"Okay. Thanks."

He hung up and bent over Dima's form. "Hey," he said softly. "Nurse said you've probably been pushing too hard and it's been building for a while. Rest, fluids, dark room, the usual. Think you can sleep?"

Dima didn't bother answering, but he fumbled a hand out from under the covers. When Rory took it, Dima pulled his hand to his mouth. Rory caught his breath but he said nothing.

It was hard to think, hard to hold any kind of rational thought. The last coherent thing in Dima's head was the thought that if he hadn't been in love with Rory before, he was well on his way there now. Then the blackness reached up to pull him down, and Dima let go gratefully.

18

It took Dima a week to recover from the migraine. He was still moving slowly when the day of the party rolled around, but he shook his head stubbornly when Rory asked if they should reschedule.

"Everyone's already coming," he said, chin jutting. "It won't be loud, they've all promised. And it's for Diego."

Rory sighed and gave in. Still, he couldn't help hovering, watching anxiously as Dima showered and pulled out clothes, until Dima snapped a glare at him.

"I'm *fine*, Rory. Go wait in the living room and try not to pout."

Rory trudged into the living room and flopped on the couch. He wasn't *pouting*, he thought, crossing his arms and scowling at nothing. He was just worried. He had a right to be worried, didn't he? Especially after what had happened last week.

Dima appeared around the corner, lips twitching as he took in the sight of Rory sprawled out on the cushions. Rory sat up abruptly.

"Oh," he said. "You look… good."

Dima smoothed the burgundy sweater over his stomach. "Thanks," he said. "So do you."

Rory shrugged that away and rolled to his feet. "Ready?"

Dima closed the distance between them and slipped his fingers behind Rory's belt, pulling him in. Rory swallowed hard. Even after several weeks of sex, he still wasn't sure how to react when Dima touched him so casually, like there was nothing to it. Dima's eyes creased with a soft smile.

"Do we have time for me to drag you in the bedroom and rip these clothes off?"

Rory couldn't help his laugh, and Dima's smile widened.

"If we're late, they'll all know *exactly* what we were doing," Rory pointed out.

"So?" Dima leaned in and kissed him, mouth soft and sweet.

"Mm—no," Rory managed, finally pulling away. "I'm *not* dealing with the chirping we'll get. Come on."

"After, then," Dima said, and followed him to the door.

HENRY'S HOUSE was spacious and welcoming, warm golden light spilling out onto the doorstep when he opened the door to greet them.

"Welcome, come in!" he said. "Any sniffles, colds, fevers lately?"

Rory and Dima exchanged a glance and shook their heads in unison.

"Sorry," Henry said, "we just have to be extra careful of Diego's immune system." Peter was clinging to his leg, blue eyes huge with curiosity.

Rory bent and put his hand up for a high five. "You've grown, Peter," he said when Peter let go of his father to slap Rory's palm. "How old are you now, fifteen?"

Peter giggled. "'M *eight*."

"How do you tell them apart?" Henry asked, shaking his head. "Even I get them mixed up sometimes."

"Professional secret," Rory said as he straightened. "Deems, this is Peter. His counterpart, William, is around here somewhere, probably plotting how to burn the house down."

"That was last month," Henry said,

swinging Peter up into his arms and gesturing Dima and Rory inside. "He's interested in poisons now."

"Oh, much better," Rory said, and Henry laughed and ushered them into the living room.

There were a few people gathered, but Rory's eyes went first to the young man in the wheelchair sitting by the fire. His dark eyes were too big for his face, hungry as they watched Rory and Dima step inside the room. Tony was sitting beside him, his own eyes worried as he watched his son.

Dima took the lead, as usual, crossing the room and putting a hand out to Diego. "Hi," he said, smiling warmly at him. "I understand we've met, but my memory's not doing so well at the moment. I'm Dima."

A smile bloomed on Diego's thin face. "I know," he said, his voice husky and low. He accepted Dima's hand. "I'm a big fan."

"Possibly your biggest," Tony added, a fond smile curving his mouth.

"And Rory," Diego said, switching his attention to him. Rory took a step forward and put out his own hand.

"Hi," he said awkwardly.

"Thank you for inviting us," Diego said. "When I heard—" He stopped to take a breath, and Tony leaned forward.

"Don't push yourself," he said quietly.

Henry reappeared then, a chair in each hand, and set them down near Diego. Rory and Dima settled themselves as Diego regained his composure.

"Do you need your oxygen?" Tony asked.

Diego shook his head, frustration flickering across his face. "I'm fine."

"I understand you played in high school," Dima said, and Diego glanced at him, eyebrows going up.

"You know about that?"

"Of course." Dima crossed his legs, the picture of ease. "I hear you were really something."

Rory watched as Dima and Diego talked, wondering what it must be like to feel so effortlessly in control. Dima always seemed to know what to say, how to say it, how to charm a smile out of the grumpiest of people. Rory couldn't even decide what *shoes* to wear some days, let alone how to talk to a stranger as if they were friends.

Without looking, Dima reached out and put a hand on Rory's knee. Rory covered it with his own, tucking his fingers into Dima's palm, and Dima squeezed, never losing the beat of conversation.

Dima made everything better. He calmed the panic that was never far from

Rory, made him believe things would work out.

Why couldn't he love Rory for real? The injustice of it choked Rory sometimes. Dima had been Rory's best friend very nearly from the day they met. He challenged Rory, made him better, made him laugh, made him *think*. He was good for him in every conceivable way. But from the beginning, he'd made it clear they were just friends and nothing more.

The year Dima had joined the team, they'd gone to the Christmas party together. And Rory had spent the entire time hoping he could catch Dima under some mistletoe so he'd have an excuse to kiss him, even laughingly. They'd only known each other for two months at that point but Rory already knew Dima would find it funny, probably kiss him back, put on a real show for their teammates, and maybe—

Instead, a few hours in, Dima caught sight of Henry in the corner with Ingrid under a sprig of mistletoe and kissed *him*, to the raucous applause and laughter of everyone in the room. Rory had forced himself to clap too, burying the disappointment deep, down where it was only a tiny whisper and it couldn't hurt him. And then later that night, he'd said the words that were carved on Rory's soul, and Rory had known. He'd never had a chance.

Dima had met Jenny a week later.

Whatever they were now, it was for Diego. It was to give a dying boy some small measure of happiness in his final days, no matter how incomplete it felt.

It wasn't real. It would never *be* real. Because Rory wasn't good enough, didn't deserve to have someone like Dima love him. His breathing shortened, vision dimming at the edges.

Dima's hand tightened abruptly on his. "Would you excuse us for a minute?" he said to Diego, and stood, pulling Rory with him. He towed him into the hall, past the kitchen and its occupants, to the far end where a small bathroom was tucked under the stairs.

Rory followed without arguing, and Dima tugged him into the bathroom, kicking the door closed behind them.

"What—" Rory's voice died in his throat as Dima pushed him up against the wall, eyes fierce in the dim room.

"What's wrong?" Dima asked, voice low.

"I—nothing."

Dima didn't look convinced. "You were about to have a panic attack. I know the signs. So tell me what's wrong."

"*Nothing*," Rory said helplessly. He *couldn't* tell Dima what was panic-looping through his brain. "I'm—I don't—Deems, please—"

Dima studied him, hands firm and body warm against Rory's. "It's shitty," he said after a minute. "Diego doesn't deserve this. I feel guilty, because I've got my life ahead of me. I can do anything I want. And he—" His breath caught.

"It's not fair," Rory whispered.

Dima nodded. "But it's good we can give him this. Show him things are changing."

He was so close. All Rory would have to do was lean forward, press their mouths together. But if he did, he thought it was possible all the longing pent up inside him would split him apart at the seams, pour out and drown them both with it.

So he held very still, closing his eyes and praying for strength.

"I wish you'd talk to me," Dima murmured. He hadn't moved, still bracing Rory against the wall, and Rory couldn't physically stop himself from dropping his head to Dima's shoulder. Dima gathered him in, arms going around him, and Rory pressed his face to the crook of Dima's neck.

"I'm s-sorry," he managed. Dima smelled good and felt better, so steady and reassuring.

"It's okay," Dima said against his hair. "You'll tell me if I can help, right?"

Rory nodded without lifting his head.

"That's all I ask." Dima kissed his hair and then took a step back. Did he look reluctant to be letting go, or was that Rory's wishful thinking? "We need to get back in there or they'll assume we snuck off for a quickie."

Rory couldn't help his grimace and Dima laughed softly.

"I know. But that's where their brains will go. Come on."

Rory followed him back down the hall, but Dima stopped him just outside the living room with a hand on his chest.

"One more thing," he said, and leaned in to kiss him.

Was his brain going to stop dead every single time, Rory wondered distantly, but the majority of his senses were focused on the feeling of Dima's mouth against his, how soft his tongue was when he licked gently at Rory's lips, asking for permission to slip between them.

Dima hummed when Rory opened for him, sounding pleased, and deepened the kiss. He brought a hand up to cradle the back of Rory's head, tilting him until he had him at the angle he wanted.

It was several minutes before Dima

eased back, just enough that he could press their foreheads together. He was out of focus from so close.

"Whatever it is," he whispered, "can you put it away for the night?"

Guilt swamped Rory. *Selfish, thoughtless, inconsiderate*—he swallowed hard. "Yeah," he managed.

"Whoops," Tony said, and they startled apart. "Sorry, boys," he continued. He was pushing Diego's chair, Diego watching them with hungry eyes. "Deo needs the bathroom."

"Dad," Diego protested. "Don't call me that."

Dima laughed and stepped out of the way, drawing Rory with him. "See you back in there," he said, and winked at Diego.

Put it away. Rory followed Dima back into the living room. He could do that. For Diego.

THE PARTY WAS SURPRISINGLY SEDATE, considering Pete had organized it. No strippers in cakes, no confetti or noise-makers, not even any alcohol. Just a lot of very large men and their respective partners making low conversation.

Diego was seated between Rory and Dima at the table, although he spent most of his time talking to Dima. That was fine by Rory, who didn't know what to talk about anyway. Would it be rude to discuss hockey, when Diego couldn't play any longer? Rory didn't have anything else *to* talk about, unless Diego wanted to discuss the horrors of Boston traffic.

As if on cue, Diego swiveled toward him, and Rory spared a moment to wonder who he'd pissed off in a past life.

"Simon Fall was all over you in that last game against the Ravens," Diego said. "How'd you keep from punching him?"

Rory huffed a startled laugh, picking up a spoon and twirling it between his fingers. "He's just your common or garden variety asshole, really. Nothing much to him when it comes down to it. And besides, Dima told me I wasn't allowed to fight." He caught Dima's eyes over Diego's head and Dima grinned.

Diego was laughing quietly. "He's really not that bad when you get to know him."

Rory did a double-take. "Wait, sorry, you know him?"

"He's the uncle of one of my best friends," Diego said. "Jack and I were always pestering him when we were little, back when he was just getting started. He used to take us pond skating every weekend before he got signed."

Rory considered that. "Huh."

"I know, hard to believe." Diego sounded wryly amused. "But he was one of the first to text me when my diagnosis was released. And he always takes me out for lunch when he comes to town. He'd deny it to his grave, but he's a good guy. Can I ask you a personal question?"

"Oh—uh... sure," Rory said.

"How did the team take it when you came out? Did you tell them together or was it separately?"

Rory caught Dima's eyes again briefly and pulled his gaze away, marshaling his thoughts. "I actually came out when Carmine did. Not his public coming out, but a few years before, when he was still with us."

"He came out to the team?"

"Yeah," Rory said softly. "You'd have to ask him why he decided to, but when he did it, I sort of... hopped on the bandwagon with him."

Diego's lips curved in a breathtakingly sweet smile. The vestiges of beauty clung to his thin frame like a shroud, in his luminous eyes and the gentle swoop of his smile. "I was so happy when I heard the news. But not as happy as when I heard about you and

Dima. Who asked who out? Can I ask that?"

"Of course," Rory said, smiling back at him. "We usually spent Christmas and New Year's together, because his family was so far away and mine—" He faltered. "Anyway, New Year's is a big deal for Russians, right? Much bigger than Christmas. So he'd get me something for Christmas and then I'd get him something for New Year's. I told him once I'd loved waking up to the smell of cardamom bread baking when I was a kid, and I think it was the second holiday we spent together, he came over to my place really early and I woke up to cardamom bread." He laughed at the memory, fondness warm in his chest.

Diego smiled with him. "And you asked him out then?"

"Well, first I had to make sure there wasn't an intruder in my apartment," Rory said wryly. There was scattered laughter around the table, and he glanced up, startled. He hadn't realized they had an audience. Dima was watching him, eyes soft, and Rory's heart lurched. "I—yeah. I guess that was when I made my move." He kept Dima's gaze, directing the next words at him. "That's when I knew he was it for me."

19

Dima kept watching him as Rory drove them home, leaning against the door, dark eyes catching the light.

"Did that really happen?" he finally asked as Rory found his parking space.

"Most of it," Rory said. He turned the car off but Dima didn't move, so Rory folded his hands in his lap. "I didn't kiss you or anything, but you came over and baked for me on Christmas. It's sort of a tradition now."

Dima made a considering noise. "That was pretty sweet of me."

Rory huffed startled laughter. "Yeah. It was." He got out, Dima following suit, and they walked to the elevator side by side, shoulders brushing. Dima seemed content to stay silent, but there was something in the silence that had Rory on edge, wondering when the shoe was going to drop.

Inside the apartment, Dima muscled Rory up against the wall, one hand resting on the base of his throat. His eyes were intent, inspecting Rory's face from just inches away, and Rory's mouth went dry.

"What—"

"Shh," Dima said, and kissed him. His mouth was warm and he tasted like the berries they'd had for dessert. Rory couldn't help the way he melted into it, so needy and desperate for the smallest scrap, for anything Dima would give him. He hated himself for being so easy, for being brought to the verge of begging by the mere touch of Dima's hand. It was pathetic, letting Dima reduce him to this—

Dima broke away. "Rory," he said sharply, and Rory blinked. "You're thinking too hard," Dima said more gently. "Focus on me, okay?"

"Yeah," Rory husked. "Sorry."

"Don't be sorry, sweetheart," Dima said, and kissed him again. This time, he curved his hand over the nape of Rory's neck, keeping him grounded, and Rory surrendered. Dima hummed, sounding pleased, and maneuvered him away from the wall, walking him backward through the apartment as he nipped along Rory's jaw.

Rory's head was spinning, fire curling up his spine even as his limbs turned to water. Dima steered them into the bedroom and backed Rory against the bed, pushing him down on it and climbing on top of him before Rory could react.

He was heavy and solid, protective armor keeping the world at bay, caging Rory in with elbows and thighs as he sealed their mouths together again.

"So beautiful," he whispered when he lifted his head.

Rory reached for him wordlessly, skin burning with his need. Dima trailed wet, sucking kisses down Rory's throat, teeth grazing over sensitive spots and making him jerk. Dima tugged his shirt aside and planted a kiss on Rory's collarbone, whispering something in Russian.

Rory felt like he was underwater, suspended, dreamlike, as Dima undressed him inch by inch, peeling layers back as if he was revealing something precious, something *treasured*, kissing the skin he bared, until Rory was naked, shaking with want and reaching for him.

But Dima shook his head, drawing back, and a whine slipped from Rory's throat. Dima wasn't going far, just easing away to pull his own clothes off, and then he was back, straddling Rory's hips again and bending to kiss him. Rory sank into it eagerly, his brain quiet for the first time in far too long. Nothing existed except the slide of Dima's skin on his, the searing hot kisses he was leaving in a trail down Rory's sternum, the press of his fingers digging into the divots in Rory's hips.

Rory worked moisture into his mouth. "Please will you fuck me, Deems?"

Dima swallowed hard. "Yeah, sweetheart. Of course."

Rory closed his eyes and Dima slid down his body.

Of all the things they'd done, and they'd done so many things, they hadn't done this yet. Rory wasn't sure why. Maybe they just hadn't gotten around to it, with everything else they were able to do, with the way Dima seemed intent on exploring every inch of Rory's body until he was a whimpering mess.

Dima was taking his time, because he always took his time, seemingly oblivious to the way Rory was falling apart, held together by desperation and the focus in Dima's dark eyes.

"Hands flat against the headboard," Dima ordered when Rory couldn't stop twitching, hips grinding in small circles to chase the feel of Dima's fingers inside him.

Rory obeyed, pushing against the frame

until it creaked as Dima went back to work. He was up to three fingers, or at least Rory thought he was. It *felt* like three, but every time he tried to focus, Dima did something devastating like nip the tendon in Rory's inner thigh, or suck a mark into the soft skin at the crease of his hip, worrying the patch with his teeth until it was livid purple and then blowing on it lightly.

"*Please*," Rory said jerkily. "I-if you don't —Deems, I'm so fucking close, come *on*."

Dima took pity on him, going to his knees and shuffling between Rory's spread thighs. He stroked one of Rory's legs, smoothing his palm over the tiny curling hairs, until Rory twisted and caught him in the ribs with his other heel.

Dima laughed out loud, catching Rory's ankle even as his head fell back, and Rory laughed with him, helpless and turned on and feeling like he was going to vibrate right out of his skin.

"Please," he repeated.

Dima's eyes softened and he bent to kiss him. "I've got you," he murmured. "You can let go, baby, I've got you."

He sat up again, positioning himself, a hand curved absently over Rory's hip as he got in position, a stitch furrowing his brow, lower lip caught between his teeth, and Rory loved him so much he had to close his eyes, afraid the truth was written there, far too obvious, too desperate for Dima to love him back.

Dima pressed inside in a single, slow stroke, pushing until he bottomed out with a shaky noise. Rory couldn't move, couldn't breathe, not a whisper of air in his lungs or thought in his head. His whole being was *Dima Dima Dima* on endless repeat as Dima ground somehow impossibly deeper, forearms shaking with the effort.

All Rory could do was lie there and take it, exposed and raw and unable to move, Dima pulling out and sliding back in. It was so much more, something terrifying in the trust Rory was placing in him, trusting Dima to make him feel good, trusting him to know what Rory *needed*.

There was something in Dima's eyes when he raised his head and looked at Rory, something blazing in the depths, fierce and hungry.

"I wish I could—" Dima broke off, shaking his head. "You deserve so much, Rory, fuck, I'm so sorry I—"

"It's okay," Rory whispered. He tucked Dima's hair behind one ear, cupping his face. *It's okay that you can't love me back. You've given me so much more than I ever hoped for.* He didn't say it. Instead he hooked an ankle around Dima's hip. "Let me feel it. *Please.*"

Dima closed his eyes briefly, then nodded and began to move.

THAT NIGHT, after they were showered and the sheets were changed, Dima curled up against Rory's back, arm over his waist and nose buried in his hair.

Neither spoke. Finally Dima pressed a kiss to the nape of Rory's neck.

"Goodnight," he whispered.

Rory stayed awake a while longer, the weight of Dima's arm a comforting prison. *How much longer can you keep this up?*

He couldn't help remembering Diego's eyes, huge and hungry, when Rory had been talking about Dima.

It didn't matter if Rory's heart broke a little more every time Dima touched him. If this was all he could do, then he'd do it, and he'd put himself back together again the best he could when it was all over.

20

HE WENT on another away trip with the team, still worried about Dima being on his own, but a little more able to put it aside and focus on his game. Everyone had heard by now, and while he got support from surprising corners, he was also getting hit more, slashed more, chirped relentlessly. He came off the ice after every shift with more bruises, his jaw aching from the way he was grinding his teeth.

It wasn't lost on Pete, but Pete couldn't be everywhere at once, and all Rory could do was try to ignore it, but it ate at him, niggling under his skin like termites chewing on his nerves. Scoring helped, though, even if he didn't have Dima to hug after.

After the game, he dragged himself to the hotel room, downed a handful of aspirin, and called Dima as he lowered himself gingerly to the bed and turned on the TV.

Dima answered almost immediately. "Hey, are you okay?"

"I'm fine," Rory said, stretching his legs out. "How's your head?"

"Sounded like a rough game," Dima said, ignoring that. "You sure you're okay?"

"Bruises, Deems," Rory said. There were highlights from a college hockey game playing. "Boston U's doing well this season. How are you?"

"Rory."

"If you won't tell me how you're feeling, why should I tell you how *I'm* feeling?" Rory snapped.

Dima took a shocked breath. "Is that— are you *mad* at me?"

"No. *No.*" Rory ground the heel of his hand against his eye socket. "Fuck. I'm sorry." Dima didn't say anything, and Rory closed his eyes. "The game was shit. I want to—I hate people sometimes, is all."

"I know," Dima said quietly. "I had lunch with Diego today. He says hi."

"Oh. How—"

"They're talking hospice." Dima sounded miserable. "I sat there and talked to him about hockey and growing up queer

and we pretended everything was normal
and he's not dying in front of me."

"Dima." Rory sat up. "Deems, I'm so
sorry. You—and I snapped at you, I—"

"Don't," Dima said. "We've both had
shitty days. But you're home tomorrow."

"It'll be late," Rory warned.

"I know." A smile softened Dima's voice.
"Too bad we're not feeling up to it or we
could have phone sex."

Rory groaned. "Pretty sure it would take
an act of God to get it up right now."

"Next time," Dima said. "Go to sleep,
Rory. I'll see you tomorrow."

21

DIEGO'S FUNERAL was held on a cold day in February, the streets treacherous with black ice and the trees stark and brittle against the gray sky. The procession to the cemetery was slow and careful on the slippery roads, Rory sitting silently next to Dima in the back of the car and not knowing what to say. Dima's mouth was tight, jaw clenched, but he reached out and took Rory's hand, halfway to the cemetery, and kept holding it after they got out and walked across the frozen grass to where the mourners were gathered.

Diego's gone, Rory thought, hating himself for the thought even as he had it. *You don't have to pretend anymore.* But he didn't let go.

The ceremony didn't take too long, the

reverend keeping his speech short and then Tony getting up.

"I know it's cold," he said, looking around at the crowd. "I won't keep you. Thank you for coming. Diego loved you all. Dima?"

Dima squeezed Rory's hand and let go to step up to the small podium. He hugged Tony, then turned to face everyone.

He hadn't told Rory he was going to say something. Rory tucked his hands in his pockets and hunched deeper in his coat.

"I didn't know Diego very well," Dima said. His voice was low but clear. "I regret that. I regret a lot of things, but Diego was a special person in so many ways. I got to spend more time with him over the past month while my team was out trying to win a Cup for him and the rest of this city. I don't know if we're going to be able to do that, but I don't think Deo really cared about that."

He clutched the podium, knuckles whitening. "He cared about love. He cared about being himself, being accepted for himself, doing what he loved and being with the people who loved *him*. I didn't know him long, but—" He swallowed. "He helped me see how important it is to be yourself, to be *true* to yourself." He found Rory and held his eyes.

Rory wasn't breathing. He shifted his feet, numb from the cold.

"The world is brighter when you're true to yourself," Dima said. "And it's a little darker today, without Deo in it."

He left the podium with no further ceremony and struck out across the grass toward the waiting cars. Rory followed without even thinking, drawn helplessly in his orbit just like always, and it didn't occur to him until he'd caught up that maybe Dima didn't want company. He stopped abruptly and Dima swung around at the scuff of his shoe on the pavement. There were tears on his face.

He went into Rory's arms without hesitation, burying his face in Rory's coat, clutching the back of it. He wasn't crying anymore, but his breathing was harsh, deep gulps of air that sounded like they hurt.

Rory held him, his own eyes stinging.

"I didn't—I barely knew him," Dima said after a minute.

"You spent almost every day with him this month," Rory said quietly.

Dima lifted a shoulder. "Not enough. Wasn't enough." He lifted his head, eyes red-rimmed. "It's not fair."

"No, it's not," Rory agreed.

"I want to go home," Dima said

abruptly. "I want—I want to get drunk and forget this day ever happened."

"You can't get drunk," Rory reminded him, wincing.

"*Goddammit.*" Dima spun away and kicked the tire of the nearest car.

"Come on," Rory said, taking his hand. "Let's get out of here, at least."

THEY DIDN'T GET DRUNK, but Rory grabbed his heaviest blanket and pulled Dima up the stairs to the roof. They curled up on the canvas sofa under the lattice that was bare of vines, Dima tucked between Rory's legs, head on his chest. The cold air stung Rory's cheeks, and he huddled deeper into the blanket, pressing his face to Dima's hair.

I love you so much. The thought was so vivid, for a minute he was positive he'd said it out loud. But Dima didn't react, body limp and heavy against Rory's.

He doesn't love you back, he reminded himself. *Not like that. He said he never would, remember? That he* couldn't.

The memory hurt as much in retrospect as it had when it had happened. More, possibly, with the weight of everything they were to each other now between them.

Dima had kissed Henry under the

mistletoe, setting him back on his feet with a flourish and a light glittering in his eyes almost like a challenge when he'd met Rory's gaze across the room. He'd been halfway to drunk, and Rory not much better off, but no amount of alcohol could erase what Dima had said to him as the party had wound down, couples leaving with their sleepy children tucked against shoulders.

They were sitting at a table in the corner. Not far from where Dima had kissed Henry, Rory had noted, not that it bothered him.

Dima's legs were stretched out, his bowtie hanging loose around his neck, watching Henry and Ingrid herd their exhausted toddlers out the door.

"Hockey wives are amazing," he said.

Rory made a noise of agreement.

"The shit they put up with," Dima continued. "I could never fall in love with a hockey player." He wasn't looking at Rory, instead staring pensively over the emptying room. His profile was lit by the twinkling lights of the Christmas tree in the corner, mouth soft.

"We're pretty gross," Rory said, trying for humor. His stomach was twisting, misery welling.

Dima hummed and took another swallow of beer. "I probably won't get married until after I retire," he said, turning the bottle in his long fingers. "But when I do, I'll find someone who's not as obsessed with this goddamn game as we are." He looked up, dark eyes catching the light. "Can you even imagine getting married? Tying yourself down like that? What if you choose wrong? What if you pick the wrong person?"

"I—" Rory shook his head. "I hadn't really thought about it, I guess."

Dima was on a roll. "But getting tangled up with a hockey player would make it that much worse, I think. Take you, for example."

Rory froze.

"You're attractive," Dima went on. "You're funny and we have great chemistry, don't we?"

"I guess," Rory said cautiously.

"We'd never work as a couple," Dima said. It had the finality of a judge slamming his gavel down, and Rory went cold to his toes, but Dima wasn't done. "I like you a lot. But being *with* you, playing *and* being together?" He shook his head. "We'd get sick of each other, I think."

"You don't know that," Rory said, barely above a whisper. His lips were numb.

Dima made a dismissive noise and drained his beer. "Too much to risk.

Besides, I don't even want to date right now." He stood and stretched, popping his back with a satisfied groan. "Got hockey to play for a while first." He held out a hand to Rory, smiling down at him. "Wanna split a cab? Your place is on the way to mine."

"FOUR YEARS," Dima said, startling Rory from his memories. "And this—us—never happened before?"

Rory snapped alert with a sickening jolt. Dima hadn't moved but Rory felt suddenly like he was on quicksand, the slightest movement dooming him.

"Well," he said cautiously, "I mean… you had a girlfriend for some of it, for one thing."

Dima sat up, shoving his hair out of his face. "But not the whole time. And you knew I liked both, right?"

Rory flinched. "I don't—can we talk about it later?"

"Yeah, of course," Dima said. "I'm sorry." He lay down and Rory pulled the blanket back into place. "I wish Diego could have come up here."

"Me too," Rory whispered. *The world is brighter when you're true to yourself.* He wanted to ask, suddenly, if Dima was going to regret this when his memories returned. He couldn't make the words come.

He dozed off despite the cold and Dima woke him around midnight, pulling him up and wrapping an arm around his waist to stumble back down the stairs to their warm bed.

22

THE NEXT DAY WAS AN OFF-DAY. Dima was well enough to use his phone for brief periods, so he did that while Rory pulled together breakfast. After, Rory settled on the couch with a book while Dima got his guitar.

He spent more time watching Dima, pick between his lips, furrow on his brow as he bent over the guitar to tune it, than he did actually reading, and when Dima struck the first chord, he gave up on pretending and put the book in his lap.

It wasn't a song he knew, the tune soft and plaintive, Dima humming occasionally. His body was curved protectively over the guitar, hair falling in his face and sunlight gilding one cheekbone. It caught Rory by surprise sometimes, just how beautiful he was.

Dima glanced up and his lips curved. Rory cleared his throat.

"I don't know that song," he said, trying to keep his tone light.

"Just something I'm playing with," Dima said, glancing back down. "Did I ever tell you I remembered Luca and Jonas, that day I visited you at practice?"

"When you had the migraine? No, you didn't tell me. Anything else come back to you?"

Dima shook his head, changing to a minor key. "I just looked at Luca and knew exactly who he was, and then Jonas was right there and same thing with him. I knew where they were from, that Luca tends to talk for them both but everyone knows to listen when Jonas does talk."

"Yep," Rory said, smiling. "Nothing about... us?"

"No." Dima stopped playing. "I keep pushing at it. It's like there's an empty space where you should be. Like... things are coming back, slowly. I remember Pete, and Jake and Oskari, or at least bits about them. But you—" He shook his head again.

"You can't force it," Rory said softly. "You have to let it come back on its own."

"What if it doesn't?" Dima demanded, hands tightening on the guitar. "What if I don't remember you? *Ever*? What if—"

"You'll make new memories of me," Rory said. His throat was tight.

"But I *want* to remember you," Dima said. He put the guitar down and crossed the room to slide onto Rory's lap, straddling his legs and cupping his face. "Don't you want that too? Don't you want me back, the old version of me?"

"I—" Rory swallowed hard. Dima was heavy on top of him, eyes soft and sad. "I'm just glad you're here at all," he said honestly.

Dima bent to kiss him. "Me too," he said when he lifted his head. "But I feel like... I know so much about you *now*, and I want to know about you *then* too, if that makes sense. See how everything... meshes, I guess."

Rory was suddenly caught with the need to get up, to move. To get away, before Dima did remember—remember how they were just friends, nothing more, never anything more, because if Rory had ever tried, ever opened his mouth and said what he'd truly felt, Dima would have looked sad, because he was a good person and he would never hurt Rory willingly, but he'd tell him it wouldn't work, that he didn't think of him that way and he was so sorry, and Rory— Rory couldn't bear that.

He pushed gently until Dima slid to the

side and then scrambled to his feet, making Dima blink in surprise.

"I'm gonna... go work out," Rory said, and Dima watched him go with a puzzled tilt to his head.

HE COULDN'T KEEP DOING this, Rory thought as he set the incline on the treadmill higher. It felt like a fever dream, vivid and over-bright and almost surreal with how perfect it was, and it was going to collapse around him like a pricked soap bubble, leaving him alone again and somehow worse off than he'd been before Dima went into the boards.

His feet thudded against the rubber mat, his heart aching in time. Sweat dripped down his face and he used the hem of his shirt to wipe it away.

Dima was going to eventually remember Rory and then he'd regret everything. Dima was going to leave him forever, because Rory wasn't enough, wasn't enough, wasn't enough. And he was going to lose him.

He missed a step and nearly fell, hauling himself back upright just in time and punching the machine's off switch with an unsteady hand.

He was the worst kind of coward, craven

and selfish and *small*, but the thought that he might have kissed Dima for the last time made him want to double over in pain. He stepped down and made for the door on unsteady legs.

HE WAS TAKEN ABACK when he left the gym and nearly ran into a young man he didn't recognize standing on the other side, hand raised as if about to knock.

"Sorry," Rory said reflexively, and stepped around him.

"Mr. O'Brien?" the young man said. He looked vaguely familiar, but Rory was pretty sure he wasn't a resident.

He hid the groan and summoned a smile as he turned. "Hey, sorry, no autographs in my own building, okay? I can't have people thinking they can just—"

"That's not—I don't want your autograph," the boy said. He looked about an inch from losing his nerve, trembling in place with his chin tipped up almost defiantly.

"No selfies either," Rory said, voice a little sharper. His legs were tired and he wanted, just once, for things to go his way.

The young man opened and closed his hands, looking utterly lost. "Please," he said, and his voice was wobbly. "I just need—"

On the verge of turning away, Rory stopped. "What?" he asked, keeping his tone gentle.

"Can I just talk to you for a minute?" the boy blurted.

Rory took a deep breath. Whoever this kid was, he clearly needed something he thought Rory could give him, and Rory had never been the type to not help if he was in a position to.

"Are you afraid of heights?" he said, and the boy's brow furrowed but he shook his head.

23

"MY NAME IS JACK HARMAN," the young man said once they were seated in the rooftop garden. "I'm a hockey player. I play for Boston College, which is part of why— anyway I'm going in the draft. I'm—" He ducked his head, looking suddenly bashful. "I'll probably go pretty early."

Rory took a closer look. "Hang on, I know you. Holy shit, you've been setting the hockey world on fire."

Jack blushed to the tips of his ears. He was slim and delicate, built for speed and agility. Rory remembered watching one of his games on the road, that night in his hotel room away from Dima, nothing else to do but watch college hockey. Jack's playing was incredible, almost Gretzky-like in the way he anticipated moves three or four steps ahead of his opponents.

"Seriously," Rory insisted. "You're gonna give Saint a run for his money sooner than you think." Another thought struck him. "Wait. Jack. Boston—fuck, are you... did you know Diego?"

Jack's shoulders drooped. "He was my best friend," he said, almost inaudible. "I was a-at his funeral, but I d-didn't think I should talk to you then."

Rory didn't remember seeing him, but he really hadn't been focused on anyone but Dima. Still. "I'm sorry," he said. "I didn't really know him but I liked him a lot. He was good people."

"Thank you," Jack said, lifting his head. "Anyway, that's not why I'm here. I mean it sort of is but not really."

Rory waited.

It took a few minutes. Jack clearly considered and discarded several options before saying, "I really love hockey."

"Me too," Rory said.

"I mean, it's the only thing I want to do," Jack said, leaning forward. "That's all there is."

Rory said nothing. He had a sinking feeling he knew what was coming.

"When I'm drafted," Jack continued, "I want to use it to come out. In honor of Diego. And because—it's time."

Rory flinched. "No," he said, knowing he sounded too harsh. "Don't do that."

"Why not?" Jack demanded. "You—you and Dima—showed me it's possible. You can be gay and play this sport, you've *proved* that. They won't be able to rescind the contract—whoever drafts me will *have* to publicly support me."

"Publicly," Rory agreed. "Have you considered what they'll say privately? What the team will do? Do you want that level of attention? Guys acting like you're checking them out or perving on them? What about the abuse you'll get on the ice, has it even occurred to you what they'll say? What they'll *do*?"

There was definitely defiance in Jack's tipped chin now as he glared at Rory.

"You do it," he snapped. "Why couldn't I?"

Rory gestured at him, briefly speechless. "*Look* at you," he finally sputtered. "You're what, a buck fifty soaking wet? You're fast, kid, but sooner or later someone's gonna catch up. You really want to be beat to a pulp, or pasted into the boards so hard you break something? You'll be *lucky* if anyone steps up to protect you, like Carmine did for me. It's not something you can count on."

Jack was regarding him with something

like compassion when he stopped. "We have to stop being afraid something bad will happen just for being ourselves," he said softly. "You taught me that."

There was a boulder in Rory's throat and he couldn't swallow around it.

"I'm scared all the time," he managed after a minute. "For me. For Dima." He *would not* cry, he told himself fiercely. "For *you,* kid."

"But you still do it," Jack countered. "Because it matters."

Because I told a lie to get into a hospital room and it all went to hell shortly thereafter.

"I'm not some kind of hero," Rory said roughly, and stood. "You do what you're gonna do, but don't go thinking the world has changed. It's just as ugly and brutal as it's ever been, and it doesn't give a shit what we do. It's gonna keep right on being ugly and brutal and we can pretend all we want that things are okay, that we deserve love, we deserve—" He cut himself off, rubbing his mouth with a trembling hand. "It doesn't matter," he whispered. "Things will never change." He had to get away before he broke down completely from the self-loathing choking him and the growing disappointment in Jack's clear gray eyes.

He took the stairs at a run, barely seeing where he was going, and careened around a corner headfirst into Dima, who must have come looking for him.

"Hey—ow—whoa," Dima said, catching him. "Rory, what's wrong?"

Rory shook his head blindly. He grabbed Dima's wrist and towed him back to the apartment.

"I don't want to talk," he snapped, shoving the door closed behind them. "I want you to fuck me. Take your clothes off."

Dima's eyebrows winged upward and Rory spun away with a growl.

"Fucking forget it," he tossed over his shoulder, and stalked for the bedroom.

Dima caught him from behind with shocking speed, shoving him up against the wall hard enough to punch the air from Rory's lungs. He went limp, face pressed to the wallpaper as Dima held him there.

"If you need something," Dima growled in his ear, "all you have to do is ask."

Rory swallowed with difficulty. "Please," he rasped. "I need—make it stop."

"Make what stop?" Dima asked, his weight keeping him in place. "Tell me, Rory."

"My head," Rory whispered, closing his eyes. "Make it stop. *Please.*"

24

SOMETHING WAS WRONG. Something was *really* wrong, and Dima didn't know what to *do,* how to fix it. Rory was trembling against him, his eyes closed and head tipped back, baring his throat. Dima had to help, had to find a way to bring his smile back. He had the feeling that if he pushed, dug for more information, Rory would shut him out completely, and he couldn't bear the thought of that.

So he nipped Rory's earlobe instead, hard enough to sting, and pushed him down the hall into the bedroom.

When Rory tried to turn for the bed, though, Dima pulled him away and steered him toward the bathroom.

"You reek," he said, still pressed up against him from behind, chin hooked over Rory's shoulder and arms around his waist. It looked like a normal lover's embrace, but Dima was holding Rory upright as Rory's legs threatened to buckle, and he was taking both their weight as he guided him into the shower. His ribs twinged, but Dima pushed it away, a distant concern. The man in his arms was his priority.

Rory wasn't speaking, eyes closed again as if he didn't care where Dima took them, or maybe he just trusted Dima enough to keep him safe. Something terrible and tender lodged itself in Dima's chest and he kissed the shell of Rory's ear.

"I won't hurt you," he said.

Rory opened his eyes at that and protest filled them. "I want—"

"I know what you want," Dima interrupted. "And you won't get it. Not that. Don't make me hurt you, Rory."

Rory's breath hitched and his head drooped.

Dima groped for the handles and turned the water on, adjusting the temperature until he was satisfied with it.

"I didn't say I wouldn't help you," he said, and pulled Rory's shirt off over his head. His shorts followed, kicked to the side in a sodden heap, and Dima let go just long enough to drag his own clothes off. Then he was back, pressing himself up against Rory's back and reveling in the slick slide of skin on skin.

"Put your hands on the wall," he ordered.

Rory obeyed. His face was damp, whether from tears or the spray, Dima wasn't sure, but he said nothing, just flattened his palms against the tile.

Dima pushed his feet apart, tugging his hips out until he was bent forward, bracing himself at an awkward angle.

"Don't move," Dima said, running a hand down Rory's flank. "No matter what I do, you keep your hands on the wall and your feet where I put them. Are we clear?"

Rory's throat worked but he nodded.

I wish I remembered you. Dima doesn't say the words. He just went to his knees.

The water slid down Rory's skin in glistening rivulets, gathering in the groove of his spine as he arched his back, and Dima was struck momentarily speechless with his beauty. Rory didn't move when Dima spread his cheeks and let the water run across his tightly furled hole.

He took his time. He rarely felt the need to hurry when it came to lovemaking, and this in particular felt too important to rush, like there were faultlines running through Rory's body and he'd shatter at the slightest wrong touch.

Rory took a breath when Dima licked a broad swath across his entrance but he said nothing, resettling his weight. Dima savored the taste, bitter, earthy, musk and salt and so uniquely, perfectly *Rory*. He explored the area thoroughly before pointing his tongue and dipping inside. Rory was tight and hot, clenching as Dima tried to press deeper, and Dima squeezed his ass cheeks sharply, a warning and a demand.

Rory took another breath and let it out slowly. His body relaxed with it and Dima squeezed again, this time approvingly. It was easier to get deeper that way, and Rory squirmed, breathing going ragged. Dima hadn't shaved in a few days, hadn't seen the need, and he knew he was leaving beard-burn on sensitive skin but he didn't slow down or back off. Instead he pushed deeper, biting and sucking at Rory's rim until it was puffy and loose around his tongue and Rory was moaning, tiny urgent noises that sounded dragged from him unwillingly.

His hands were still on the wall, Dima saw when he leaned back to check, and catch his breath. Rory's head was drooping between his arms and his cock hung heavy and flushed, but still he didn't move, and pride flashed through Dima.

"Doing so good," he crooned, and rewarded him with a few quick, firm strokes of his shaft before going back to work. He worked a finger in alongside his tongue this time, knowing that without lube to ease the way it had to burn, like a fire in Rory's core. There was a bottle of lube on the shower shelf but Dima didn't reach for it. Instead he soothed the sting away with his mouth, sucking wet, sloppy kisses into Rory's skin as he pumped his finger in and out, slow and unrelenting.

Rory almost moved when he added a finger, back arching abruptly against the rough stretch, but he caught himself at the last minute and stayed in position. Dima hummed approval into his skin and Rory made a noise like a sob.

"Please," he said raggedly. "Dima, please, I don't deserve it but I need—"

Dima's mouth was busy and he couldn't say what he wanted to say. *You* do *deserve it. You deserve everything. Whatever you think you did, it's not as bad as you think.*

He rocked to his feet and grabbed the lube, suddenly unable to draw it out any longer, hands shaking with need as he gripped Rory's hip and lined himself up. Rory was tight around him as he worked his way inside, inch by inch until he was buried to the hilt in his silken heat. Dima gave him time to adjust, hands running restlessly over every inch of skin he could reach. He slipped his fingers into Rory's curls, definitely long enough to get a good handful, and pulled.

Rory went easily, eyes half-lidded with pleasure. He let Dima pull his head to the side and suck a mark into his throat, rocking his hips in a wordless plea for more.

Dima gave it to him, fingers digging into his hip bones hard enough he knew they'd bruise as he ground deep over and over, finding the perfect angle so he was hitting the bundle of nerves at Rory's center on every pass and Rory was choking on his moans, scrambling to keep his feet where Dima had put them.

"Come on, then," Dima said in his ear. He gripped Rory's cock and stroked, a staggered counterpoint to his measured thrusts. "Come for me," he growled. "Let me see it, come on."

The noise Rory made was gut-deep, wrenched from him as he seized and shuddered and spilled, suddenly vise-tight around Dima's cock and pulling his own orgasm from him in a rush, bliss sparking his nerves alight.

They came down slowly, the water still pouring from the shower and their shaky breathing the only sound in the small room. Dima slid out and Rory made a pained noise as he slipped free, come pearling at his entrance and dripping down his leg.

Dima soothed him wordlessly, gathering his come and rubbing it into Rory's skin in gentle circles. *Mine,* he told him with every stroke of his thumb. He pulled him upright and gently maneuvered him into the spray to clean him off. Rory let his head droop onto Dima's shoulder, all the tension gone from his body, and Dima didn't say a word, afraid to break the fragile peace.

He didn't bother with clothes, urging Rory out of the bathroom once they were mostly dry and guiding him into the bed. Rory went easily, limbs loose and pliant, and Dima plastered himself against his back. Under the covers, it was going to be too hot in no time at all, but it was all he wanted right now, to be connected to Rory at every possible point until it was impossible to see where one ended and the other began.

"Can you talk about it?" he asked, nose brushing the nape of Rory's neck and the damp curls there.

Rory shook his head. "Dima—"

"Shh," Dima said. He kissed the bump of Rory's spine. "It's gonna be okay."

He wasn't sure if Rory believed him, but he didn't say anything else. Dima fell asleep to the sound of his breathing.

He woke up to an empty bed, and he knew by the stillness around him that the apartment was empty too.

There was a text waiting for him. *Errands to run before practice. Back for nap before game.*

Dima considered the ceiling. His ribs *hurt*, the result of way too much strenuous activity. He was pretty sure that's the only reason it was hard to breathe deeply.

He texted Rory back. *Feeling okay?*

Yes, was all he got in response.

Dima frowned at the phone but didn't push it. He'd talk to him before Rory's nap. Face to face was better anyway.

He was halfway through making breakfast when a random image floated into his mind. It was Rory, wearing his uniform, smiling. God, Dima loved his smile, the way it started in his eyes and radiated outward before it ever reached his mouth.

He was smiling at Dima, head tilted to one side, waiting as Dima got closer. Right before they bumped into each other, Rory opened his arms and folded Dima into them as Dima draped his around Rory's neck. They were laughing as they clung to each other, surrounded by twenty thousand fans.

The egg in Dima's hand slipped free and

shattered on the floor. He jumped and swore, recalled to himself, and bent to clean it up.

That had been a memory. He *remembered* that day. He'd gotten first star of the game, and he'd felt the pride beaming off Rory long before he reached him, radiating out and wrapping Dima in warmth and love, and Dima remembered *viscerally* the feeling of having to stop himself from kissing him at center ice.

He wracked his brain for more, searching frantically for something, *anything* else. But nothing came up, and he'd abruptly had enough of the self-control, of the waiting. He grabbed his phone and opened the YouTube app.

Three hours later, he'd forgotten all about food. He was curled up on the couch, watching games, highlights, interviews, gifs, everything he could find of him and Rory together, on the ice and off it. His head ached dully but he barely even noticed, cueing up the next video. He was so absorbed in what he was doing that he didn't hear the front door opening, and he was nearly startled off the couch when Rory demanded, "What are you doing?"

Dima blinked, lifting his head and trying to focus. There were several Rories in front of him at first, and it took a minute for them to resolve into one, currently glowering at him from the doorway.

"I remember you," Dima said without preamble, and the anger on Rory's face dissolved into shock and something oddly like panic before it was replaced by the most patently false smile Dima has ever seen.

"That's great, Deems!" he said. Dima rolled off the couch and approached him. Rory held his ground, but his eyes were wary. "Is it all back?" he asked.

Dima shook his head and a wave of nausea hit him. "No," he said, ignoring it. "Bits and pieces. I've been watching videos of you. Us. Rory—" He cut himself off as a spike of pain jolted through his temples and he doubled over, clutching his head.

Rory grabbed his shoulder, steadying him. "Fuck, Dima, what'd you do?"

Dima opened his mouth to answer and his stomach suddenly twisted violently and he vomited all over the floor. Rory swore and jumped back, and Dima went to his knees, still retching helplessly. He heard running footsteps dimly, and then Rory was there again, a hand under his elbow as he urged him to his feet. He shoved a bowl into Dima's arms when they were upright.

"Use that if you need to throw up again," he ordered. "Watch your step."

He guided Dima out of the entryway

and down the hall to the bedroom as Dima clutched the bowl and his head pounded in time with his heart, a sick, vicious throbbing that wrapped around his skull and buried its claws deep in his brain.

In the bedroom, Rory got him into the bed, then disappeared again briefly. He was back almost immediately with a wet washcloth, which he used to wipe Dima's face and mouth.

"'M so sorry," Dima slurred.

"Shut up," Rory said, but there was no heat to the words. "Can you keep medicine down?"

"Can try."

He took the pills Rory gave him, but it was no use—two minutes later his stomach rejected them and he barely grabbed the bowl in time.

"Okay," Rory said softly. He took the bowl from Dima's trembling hands once he was sure the heaving had stopped and carried it into the bathroom to empty and rinse it. "Lie down," he said when he was back.

"Threw up all over your hardwood floor," Dima mumbled, curling up on his side with the bowl tucked into the crook of his elbow.

"It's seen worse," Rory said. "Besides, it could have been carpet." He crouched by the bed and stroked Dima's hair off his face. His eyes were soft with worry. "You pushed yourself too hard," he said, and Dima scowled.

"I wanted to *know*," he said mutinously. He reached out and touched Rory's cheek. "I miss you. I miss...." He squeezed his eyes shut, groping through the pain for the word. "I miss knowing you," he said, and Rory took a wounded breath.

"God, *Dima*."

Dima turned his face into the pillow. His ribs were stabbing him with every breath, no matter how shallow, and the pain in his head was flooding the rest of his body, making him feel tainted somehow, sick to the core.

"Try to sleep," Rory whispered. "I'll be right here if you need anything."

"You always are," Dima mumbled, and let go.

HE DIDN'T REALLY SLEEP—HE was hurting too much for that. But he drifted, dimly aware of Rory moving around the room, tidying up and then changing out of his street clothes, the dresser opening and closing near-silently. He left for a few minutes—presumably to clean up Dima's mess, but he was back quickly, sliding into the bed beside him.

Dima didn't open his eyes but he wriggled backward until he was pressed up against Rory's side. Rory put a hand on his hip, squeezing gently.

"How are you doing?" he murmured.

Dima grunted in response, and Rory huffed a soft laugh.

"Fair enough. I'm gonna sleep, but if you need me, wake me up."

"I love you, Rory," Dima said, only half-aware of what he was saying.

Rory froze momentarily. "Yeah, Deems, I love you too," he said after a minute. His tone was light, almost careless. Like it didn't *matter*.

No, Dima wanted to protest. *I* love *you. Like, really love you. And I think you love me too.* But sleep was finally pulling at him, his consciousness fraying at the edges like a badly mended quilt, and he gave up. He'd tell him later, when he could actually string words together. He'd make him believe it. Make him *see*.

25

When he woke up again, Rory and the migraine—or at least the worst of it—were both gone. And his memories were back.

Dima sat bolt upright, wincing briefly but discarding the pain as vignettes flashed through his mind.

"Hi," Rory says, putting out a hand. "Rory O'Brien. Welcome to Boston."

Dima likes his smile immediately, the warmth of his brown eyes and the smile lines around them. He likes Rory's long nose and powerful build and dark, curly hair, too, very much.

HE'S APPROACHING Rory after a win, flush with victory, suffused with delight. He can't help moving to the music, biting his lip and looking at Rory from under his lashes as he grins. Rory just laughs as Dima slings an arm around his shoulders and lets his weight hang off him. Rory takes it without missing a beat. He always does.

THEY'RE ON THE BENCH, and Rory is angry. A botched goal, maybe a missed call, but he's steaming, glaring at the ice as if it's personally responsible. Dima can't help it—he slides closer, wraps an arm around him, and bonks their helmets together gently, a reminder that he's there, that Rory's not alone. Rory's expression doesn't change, but he relaxes against him ever-so-slightly.

DIMA'S SCORED his sixth of the season, only three games in, and he's exhausted from the shift but still zinging with happiness. Rory slides closer and leans in to take Dima's hand, right there in front of twenty thousand fans. He squeezes his fingers gently as he tells him how proud he is of him, forced to shout to be heard but the moment still close and intimate,

just the two of them. Dima can't help the smile. He doesn't let go until Rory does.

THEY EMBRACE AFTER A WIN, and Dima tucks his face into the crook of Rory's neck as Rory talks in his ear, arms solid and strong around him. Dima doesn't care that twenty thousand people are watching. This is all that's important—Rory's focus one hundred percent on him as he holds him tight.

"So DIMA'S pretty fucking hot, eh?"

Dima stops on his way past the partially ajar door at the sound of his name. It's the first Christmas party since he was traded, he's working on an excellent buzz, and he's thinking seriously about 'accidentally' ending up under the mistletoe with Rory if he can manage it. But first, he needs a quick bathroom stop.

He's not sure who speaks—he hasn't memorized everyone yet. But he absolutely recognizes Rory's light baritone in response.

"I guess," he says, sounding bored.

Dima flinches.

"Oh c'mon," the other speaker says. "You're not into that? Seriously?"

"Dunno what to tell you, man," Rory says. "He's a great guy, but he's just not my type."

"That's bullshit," the other man says. "I've seen you checking him out."

"Just because he has a great ass doesn't mean I want to date him," Rory snaps.

Dima hears footsteps down the hall and bolts before he's caught lurking like a creep.

He kisses Henry under the mistletoe, well past buzzed, and doesn't look at Rory when he lets him go, rumpled and laughing. Instead he turns his attention to getting well and truly drunk.

He meets Jenny three days later. She's tiny and soft and smells like flowers and she's everything Rory isn't, and Dima puts every thought of Rory as anything more than his friend firmly out of his mind.

"Rory," Dima said out loud, tasting the word in his mouth. "Goddammit, *Rory*." He checked the time—an hour to puck drop. He didn't have long, not with the way Boston traffic tended to move.

He scrambled out of bed and swayed as a wave of lingering pain swamped him. It was nowhere near as bad—no nausea, only a faint ache in his skull. It was bearable, he decided, and turned to the closet and the suit Rory had brought him a few weeks before.

He took the fastest shower of his life, scraped his hair into a club at the base of his skull, and got dressed. He grabbed the first tie he found in Rory's closet and stuffed it in his pocket as he hunted for shoes. As an afterthought, he grabbed a snapback and the sunglasses Rory gave him just in case. Then he was out the door.

On the way to the arena, he put the tie in a quick Windsor knot. All he could think about was Rory's face when Dima had said his memory was back, his tone of voice when he'd said he loved him too.

Had it all been a lie? Had he been pretending the whole time, *humoring* poor Dima, who'd lost his memory and didn't know better than to want a man who didn't want him back?

Dima clenched his fists and then forced himself to relax. He had to talk to him. If he could just look Rory in the face and *ask* him, he knew he'd get the truth one way or the other.

His knee jigged restlessly and he stared blindly out the window at the passing cars. The migraine was nearly gone, just lingering around the edges, and he felt almost normal, except for the confusion tinged with fury burning in his gut. If Rory had been *indulging* him, faking... *any* of what they've been doing, Dima wasn't a hundred percent he was going to be able to forgive him.

The car was going so slowly. They weren't going to make it before warmups, let alone puck drop. Dima gritted his teeth and didn't ask the driver to go faster or break any laws.

When they finally arrived, Dima directed him to the players' entrance and tipped him generously. There were very few people around, and only arena staff, Dima was relieved to see. No eagle-eyed journalists hungry for a story on hand to grab him and ask him uncomfortable questions.

He stopped briefly to talk to the guard, whose face lit up at the sight of him. Dima forced himself to smile, to ask after his family, but internally he was chafing, desperate to get through the doors and find Rory. Finally, he was waved inside and he jogged down the hall, ignoring the pain in his ribs. Loud music thumped through the underbelly of the arena, vibrating through Dima's teeth. He checked the time again and his heart sank. They were in warmups now. He wouldn't have a chance to talk to Rory before the game started.

The equipment manager in the locker room was delighted to see him and now that there was no point in hurrying, Dima took a minute to talk to him, and the others coming in and out of the room, all happy to welcome him back and ask him how he was feeling. He answered the question over and over, smiling at them, but his mind was on Rory, who must be out on the ice right now.

Eventually he managed to excuse himself and slip out to the rink. There was a spot by the Zamboni doors where, if he kept the sunglasses and cap on and didn't draw attention to himself, he should be able to watch without being interrupted.

If anyone did recognize him, they left him alone. The Otters were a swirling mass of blue on his end of the ice, Henry in net. Oskari was off to the side, stretching. Luca, Jonas, and Pete flashed by in a clump, moving too fast for Dima to see their expressions, and then there was Rory, dropping to stretch next to Oskari. There was a smile on his face and he didn't seem to have a care in the world.

Dima balled his fists and took a deep breath. He couldn't confront Rory before the game. He *couldn't*, it would be far too upsetting for Rory, who needed his focus to play well. Especially—Dima squinted to see the other side of the ice and groaned internally—against the fucking *Racers*.

He glanced at the clock—warmups were

almost over. Rory hadn't seen him yet, and that was good. Dima retreated, up the stairs to a corner of the players' box where he hopefully wouldn't be caught on camera but he could still watch. He greeted the occupants—several players' wives and a few businessmen who owned stock in the Otters, and settled in to wait, rehearsing what he was going to say when it was time.

26

Rory hated the Racers. *That's not fair,* he amended silently as the centers took up position for the initial puck drop. Plenty of Racers were decent people, with wives and kids and good lives.

Not Dean Jefferson, though. Rory glared at him from his position off to the side as the referee waited for them to get ready. It would be better for the world if Dean Jefferson didn't exist, Rory felt strongly. Even if he *hadn't* run Dima into the boards, he was a particularly nasty piece of work and Rory wanted no part of him. The fact that he was an excellent hockey player just made Rory madder. In a perfect world, bad people wouldn't be good at things, especially not Rory's favorite thing *in* the world—besides Dima.

Jefferson caught Rory's glare and smirked.

Then the puck dropped and they were off.

It was chippy from the very beginning. Jacob got taken out by a trip that had him landing on his leg at a bad angle—he had to be helped off the ice, his normally smiling mouth tight with pain.

Luca nearly got run into the boards but he twisted away at the last second and avoided the collision.

A Racer scored on Oskari, then another sank one a minute later.

Everywhere Rory looked, Jefferson was there. Stealing the puck, getting in the way, spoiling plays and *smiling*, always smiling, that mean, sharp-edged slicing grin that said *someone's going to get hurt and I hope it's you.*

ARMY JUMPED the faceoff and got waved out of the circle. Rory was pulled in, and he settled himself across from Jefferson, who was *still* smiling.

"How's your *husband*?" he asked conversationally as they readied themselves.

Rory ignored him. Why was the ref taking so long?

"Thought I saw him up in the box earlier," Jefferson continued. "Nice of him to come support you and all that."

"He's at home," Rory said reflexively, and cursed himself for reacting.

"Trouble in paradise already?" Jefferson said, false sympathy radiating off him. "Have you tried therapy?"

"What the fuck ever, man," Rory snapped before he could stop himself. "At least I still have all my hair."

Jefferson opened his mouth to say something and the ref *finally* dropped the puck.

Rory was off-balance, too slow, and he lost, of course he did. Jefferson knocked it between his own feet and back to his d-man, and the race was on again. Rory charged down the ice, cursing himself. He couldn't look at the Otters' box, couldn't take the time right now to see if Jefferson was right or just trying to get in his head— odds were decent it was the latter but Rory couldn't be *sure*.

He paced Army, who was driving toward the net with the puck, on the far wall, watching in case Army decided to send it to him.

Was Dima there? Had he come to the game, after—after everything? After they had mind-blowing sex because he was having a mental breakdown, Rory amended. And after *that*... he still couldn't believe

Dima had told him he loved him. He'd told himself Dima meant it platonically, that it hadn't been what Rory had wanted to hear for years, that it wasn't *real*.

But he wasn't *sure*, and as much as he wanted to know, he also just wanted things to stay the way they were. Dima may have wanted his memories back, but Rory loved it like this, loved *him* like this—always hungry for Rory, openly affectionate, never hesitating to show how he felt. He didn't want to go back to pretending they were nothing more than friends.

Army lost the puck and Rory dove for it but the Racer in his way neatly avoided him as the play swung back the other direction.

Rory headed for the bench, exhausted, and flopped onto it. From here, if he twisted, he could see the box, but the only people visible were a few wives talking to a couple of businessmen, judging from the suits. He didn't see Dima anywhere.

A flash of dark hair caught his eye from the corner of the box. Rory strained but he couldn't see anything else, and then it was time for him to get back on the ice.

It went wrong almost immediately. Rory hit a divot that bobbled him as he was reaching for the puck and he missed it by a scant inch as one of the Racers whipped it away. Rory gave chase, gritting his teeth, and he was in the perfect position to watch helplessly from too far away as Jacob stole it from the forward and then Jefferson, *fucking Jefferson*, elbowed Jacob in the head from the side and stole the puck back.

Jacob's head jerked and his knees gave out. He crumpled in what felt like slow motion, one hand going up to his head as he fell, and then Rory was past him and colliding with Jefferson.

They went down in a pile of flailing limbs, Jefferson spitting something furious. Rory felt a hard tug in his lower right leg but he ignored it, hauling back on his knees and punching Jefferson's despised face with every ounce of fury and frustration and terror he'd felt over the past several months.

Jefferson's head snapped back and blood bloomed. He did his best to hit back, but Rory had height and reach on him, and all he had to do was lean back when Jefferson swung wildly. He peppered Jefferson with several more hard, quick jabs, knowing he had scant seconds before the referees arrived, punctuating them with a solid crack to his ribs.

"How's it feel?" he snarled, grabbing Jefferson's jersey and hauling him up off the ice until they were nose-to-nose. "I hope I broke your fucking ribs, you piece of—"

Someone grabbed his arm and dragged

him backward, up and off. Rory stumbled and several linesmen caught him simultaneously, hauling him back up.

"I'm fine, I'm *fine*," he snapped, trying to shake them off.

"You're fucking bleeding out, you absolute *moron*," the referee shouted, and Rory looked down to see a pool of blood rapidly spreading around him.

"Oh," he said blankly, and dizziness hit him. He swayed, steadied by the hands on him, and then the EMTs were there with a stretcher and they were wrestling him onto it despite his protests. He was fine, he told them, the cut wasn't that deep, but they ignored him, carrying him off the ice and down the tunnel.

Truth be told, he *wasn't* feeling that great. He was getting dizzier, exhaustion sitting like an anchor on his chest making it hard to breathe, and he gulped for air in sharp, short pants.

The paramedics reached the ambulance and loaded his stretcher into it in one smooth, practiced motion. Rory rolled his head on the pillow, grasping weakly for the nearest person's wrist.

"Need to tell Dima," he managed.

"Hold up!" someone shouted over the sound of running feet, and then Dima was *there*, climbing into the ambulance with frantic worry writ large all over his expressive face.

"You can't be here," someone snapped.

"*Please*," Dima said, not taking his eyes off Rory, who couldn't believe he was really there. He was dreaming, or maybe just hallucinating.

"Dima," Rory slurred, and passed out.

27

THE PARAMEDICS LET Dima ride with them to the hospital under protest, ordering him to stay in the corner and out of the way. Dima obeyed, squeezing himself into the space and making himself as small as possible.

Rory was far too pale, five o'clock shadow stark against milk-white skin. His eyes were closed, head lolling on the pillow. The paramedics were busy cutting his pants off, stripping him down to get to the injury, and Dima swallowed hard when he saw it. The gash was in his calf, and it was *deep*, blood soaking through the layers of Rory's uniform and still pumping sluggishly, coating the paramedics' hands as they worked to get the wound site closed. One of them was swearing, low and steady, in Spanish—Dima caught the occasional obscenity and agrees wholeheartedly with the sentiment.

"Posterior tibial artery," one of the medics said, and the other grunted agreement. "Roll him over, I can't reach the source of the bleeding from here."

They flipped Rory, one of them turning his head so he didn't suffocate in the pillow, and went right back to work.

Don't you dare fucking die on me, Dima thought with all his might, willing the sentiment into Rory's head. *If you die, I'll fucking kill you myself, you hear me?*

Rory's lips were too white. Sweat stood out on his face. Dima loved him so much he thought he might throw up from the fear choking him.

The ambulance was flying, tossing them against the walls when it careened around corners, but Dima barely noticed, too focused on the way Rory's hand dangled limply off the stretcher.

Please, he thought. He didn't know who it was to. Anyone who was listening, probably. *Don't let him leave me. I'm not ready.*

THE RIDE to the hospital was the longest stretch of Dima's life. He hadn't made a sound the entire way, and when the ambulance was parked and they were sliding Rory out, one of the medics visibly startled at the sight of him, then jerked his chin as if to say *come on then.*

Dima unfolded himself and followed, keeping a foot behind as the nurses met the stretcher and took over. One peeled off and stopped him with a hand on his chest.

"Sir," she said firmly, "sir, you can't go in there, I'm sorry."

Rory was disappearing behind a curtain, shouted orders blending into white noise in Dima's head.

"Please, I—" He swallowed hard.

"Are you family?" the nurse asked, eyes gentle but stance implacable.

A sense of fatality settled over Dima's shoulders. "I'm his husband," he whispered, and he would have laughed at the irony but nothing about this was funny.

The nurse clucked sympathetically and guided him to a private waiting room. "Do you have anyone who can come be with you while he's in surgery?" she asked.

Everyone Dima could think of was currently at the hockey game. He shook his head briefly.

"I'll be fine."

The nurse hesitated but Dima just dropped into a plastic chair, and finally she nodded. "The doctor will find you as soon as they're done."

Then she was gone, and Dima was alone with his thoughts. He put his head in his hands. All he could see when he closed his eyes was Rory's face, slack and unconscious. *Rory*.

Dima loved him. He knew that with a stark, unmoving certainty. He'd loved him for years. He'd love him for the rest of his life, and there was nothing he could do about it. Nothing he *wanted* to do about it. Even if he moved on, went back to Finland, met someone else—it wouldn't matter. Some part of him would be in love with Rory O'Brien until his dying day, and Dima wouldn't want it any other way. Rory made him better, stronger. He braced Dima when Dima thought he didn't have the strength to face something. He fought for him—with him—beside him. He was *part* of Dima, irrevocably entwined in his life in every way. It wasn't the wild, heady rush of new love, not the chaotic waterfall of lust and infatuation, but stronger, steadier, a deep river that wouldn't be swayed from its course.

And if he didn't love Dima back, didn't feel the same way—Dima didn't know what he'd do. He rubbed his face and sat up as the door opened and Henry stepped inside.

"*Hank*." Dima met him halfway across

the room and Henry hauled him into a hard embrace.

"Hey kid," he said softly. "How's he doing?"

Dima didn't want to let go, but he forced himself to, taking a reluctant step back. "He's in surgery. The medics said something about his artery. I don't—" He dragged in air, pushing the panic away again. "What are you doing here? The game's not over yet. Is it?"

Henry shook his head and guided him to a chair. "Game's almost over and it's not going to make a difference. The ebug's already dressing and Coach told me to come be with you. The others will be here after the game."

"Jacob," Dima said suddenly, sitting up straight. "Is he okay?"

"He's fine," Henry assured him. "Passed concussion protocol with flying colors. He was back on the ice before I left. I'm more worried about you."

Dima shook his head. "I'm fine."

"How's your head? Your ribs?"

"Fine," Dima repeated impatiently. "Seriously, Hank, don't fuss. I'm not the one in *surgery* right now."

Henry patted his knee. "Rory told me your memories were coming back in bits and pieces. How's that going?"

"I remember pretty much everything," Dima said, and leaned back in the chair, resting his head against the wall.

"Everything?" Henry sounded curious and encouraging.

Dima closed his eyes. "There are still a few gaps. But Rory—I definitely remember him."

"Do you want to talk about it?" Henry asked gently.

"Is he just humoring me?" Dima spat, sitting up again. Henry's eyebrows shot up, but Dima wasn't done. "Am I a pity project to him? 'Poor Dima, doesn't remember anything, he only wants sex because he doesn't realize I don't feel the same way'?"

Henry's eyebrows notched even higher. "Um."

"If he just went along with it because he didn't want to hurt me by saying no, I'll—" Dima's hands were shaking. He shoved them under his thighs to hide it. "Hank, I need to *know*."

But Henry shook his head. "No. I'm sorry, Dima, but this needs to come from Rory. It's not for me to answer."

Dima slumped in the chair again, staring at the wall.

"One thing I can tell you, that I think you already know if your memories are back, is that he really does love you," Henry continued.

Dima rolled his head to look at him. "The way I love him?"

Henry sighed. "Chin up, kid. He'll be out of surgery soon and you can ask him yourself."

Dima crossed his arms and scowled, and Henry patted his knee again.

It was over an hour before the doctor arrived, pulling her mask off and tucking it in her pocket as she stepped through the door. She introduced herself as Dr. Collins, and she had a soft accent Dima couldn't quite place.

"The surgery went well," she said with a tired smile. "He lost quite a lot of blood, but the procedure itself was fairly simple. He'll need rest and plenty of fluids once he's released, and expect him to have a great deal of pain at first—that cut was pretty deep."

"Can I see him?" Dima asked, nearly vibrating in place.

"He's asking for you," the doctor said, smile widening. "Don't expect coherence though—he's very out of it."

Dima nodded, just barely keeping

himself from bouncing on his toes. "Please—"

Dr. Collins motioned. "Follow me."

Dima threw a look at Henry on his way out the door. "Tell the team," he said, and Henry flapped a hand, shooing him off.

THEY DIDN'T HAVE FAR to go before the doctor opened a door and ushered him into a room. It was dark, the only lights set in the ceiling around the bed, so Rory lay in a halo of pale yellow halogen. He was turning his head restlessly on the pillow, hands opening and closing.

"Dima," he said. "Dima, please—"

Dima slipped around the doctor and crossed the room in two quick steps. "I'm here," he said, taking Rory's hand in both of his. "Hey, hey Rory, I'm here, can you hear me?"

Rory frowned, brow knitting. He was still far too pale, and it made Dima's heart hurt.

"I'm sorry," Rory said, and Dima's throat closed up.

"Don't be sorry," he managed. "You haven't done anything wrong."

Rory shook his head, loose and uncoordinated. "Made you think—" He opened his eyes but they were unfocused and confused. "Dima," he repeated. "Dima, I'm sorry."

"It's okay," Dima whispered, fighting back tears. "Whatever it is you did, or th-think you did... it's okay. Rory, I'm here."

Rory sighed and relaxed, his face going slack as he fell back into sleep. Dima stayed where he was, watching him, his heart aching.

28

RORY CAME BACK to consciousness slowly, his world fading in around the edges a few pixels at a time. He heard the beep of the monitors, soft voices outside the room, smelled antiseptic and clean cotton, felt the thin, rough blanket under his hand.

His eyes were heavy and felt like sandpaper when he blinked them open, but he managed. The first thing he saw was Dima sitting in the chair beside the bed, folded forward at the waist with his head on the mattress by Rory's thigh. His eyes were closed and he was sound asleep, judging by the slow, steady breaths.

Rory watched him for a few minutes, feeling more and more alert. If this was the last time he'd get to see Dima soft and unguarded like this, he wanted to savor it, so he took his time tracing the lines of his face with his eyes, memorizing the details yet again.

Dima stirred and lifted his head, knuckling sleep from his eyes. Awareness filled them fast when he saw Rory gazing at him, and he jolted to his feet, knocking the chair backward.

"You're awake," he said stupidly.

"Well, it's not the fantasy I usually have, so I'm guessing so," Rory said.

Dima didn't smile, and Rory's stomach dipped.

"How are you?" Dima asked.

Rory evaluated. "Pretty okay," he finally decided. "But I can't feel my leg. I still have it, right?"

"Jefferson's skate severed an artery," Dima said. His face was still unreadable, but he was watching Rory so intently that Rory felt like a bug under a microscope. "They had to operate, but the doctor said you should regain full motion with proper rehab."

Rory made an aborted movement, reaching for him and pulling back. "Dima—"

"I know you just woke up but we need to talk," Dima said flatly, and dread curdled Rory's stomach.

"Or we could *not* do that," he suggested.

"I remember nearly everything," Dima

said, ignoring him, and the dread turned into a solid lump. "I remember you, Rory. I remember *us*."

This was it, then. This was how it ended. With Dima staring at him, hard and implacable, his hair a mess from sleep and lines on his face from the sheet, and Rory loved him so much he couldn't breathe, and he was going to lose him.

"I'm sorry," he said, or tried to say, but his voice wouldn't cooperate and it came out small and cracked.

"You keep saying that," Dima snapped. "When you first woke up after surgery and now—what are you sorry for, Rory? What did you do that's so awful?"

Rory struggled to breathe. "I—I let you think—"

"You let me think what?" Dima asked. There was no give to his voice.

Rory squeezed his eyes shut. There was nothing for it. He had to confess, and accept the consequences.

"I let you think it didn't matter," he whispered.

"*What* didn't matter?" Dima demanded. He sounded like he had in the hall, when Rory had asked him to make his head stop. "Use your fucking words, Rory, I'm *done* with guessing at shit."

"Us!" Rory shouted, and Dima's mouth

snapped closed. "I let you think it was just sex, okay? That it didn't *mean* anything to me, it was just—" He took a ragged breath. "I tried to pretend I wasn't in love with you, okay? Is that what you want to hear? I've been in love with you for fucking *years* and I'm sorry, I tried not to be because of what you said but I couldn't *help* it, and then they wouldn't let me in to see you and I was so scared, Dima, I thought you were dying and I'd never see you again, so I lied and said you were my husband so they'd let me in and then everything just—spiraled. I didn't know how to tell you, not when you didn't remember. It felt like… taking advantage. Or—I don't know. I'm a coward, okay? But I couldn't *tell* you."

Dima was standing very still. When Rory ran out of breath and finally shut up, he didn't move, just staring at him. Rory couldn't figure out the expression on his face, and that scared him more than anything. He'd been able to read Dima's emotions since a few months after they met.

Without a word, Dima spun and left the room. The door shut quietly behind him, more final than if he slammed it.

Alone, Rory covered his face. He'd *known* it would end badly, that he was going to lose Dima in every way imaginable, but he hadn't realized just how much it would hurt to watch him leave. He took deep breaths, willing himself not to cry, but it was no use—the tears were welling anyway, spilling down his cheeks.

The door opened again, and Rory looked up, expecting to see a nurse or maybe the doctor.

Dima was standing there.

"I am so mad at you," he said, and Rory flinched in spite of himself.

"I'm sor—"

"No," Dima interrupted. "You just shut up for once and let me talk. You lied to me."

"I didn't m—"

"You're right, you let me think it was casual. That it wasn't *real.* Did you think I couldn't handle it if I knew how you felt? Could you really not trust me even that much?"

Rory felt like he'd been hit. He couldn't come up with words.

Dima's eyes were sparking with fury, liquid in the dimly lit room. *He's so beautiful,* Rory thought fleetingly.

"Four years," Dima spat. He shoved a hand through his hair. "Four years, and I've been in love with you for at least three of them, and *you lied to me.*"

All the oxygen was gone from the room. Rory gaped helplessly at Dima, who glared back at him, implacable.

"I—I don't—"

"You were just never going to tell me, is that it? Just go through life suffering nobly because *poor Rory, in love with someone who doesn't love him back.* Did you *ever* consider telling me how you felt?"

"Every fucking day!" Rory yelled back, stung beyond reason. "You didn't *want* me, Dima! I wasn't going to force you to have to tell me you didn't feel the same way and make it awkward between us, okay?"

"How do you know I didn't want you?" Dima asked, his tone low and dangerous. He'd moved farther into the room, but he was still at least three feet from the bed.

"Because you said so!" Rory flung at him. Dima blinked, taken aback. "You *said* so," Rory continued. "You said you could never be with a hockey player. With *me*, specifically. You said—" The pain choked him and he took a ragged breath. Dima looked utterly baffled. "I guess that part hasn't come back," Rory said bitterly. "Lucky you. I remember it just fine. You said you liked me but that if we were ever together it would never work, we'd get sick of each other."

"When?" Dima asked, and he sounded strangely urgent.

"I—that first Christmas party," Rory managed.

"But *when* did I say it?" Dima pressed.

"After—I mean… you kissed Hank. It was after that. The party was basically over, we were one of the last ones there, and you —" Rory gestured.

"'Dima's pretty fucking hot, eh?'" Dima said, clearly imitating someone. He cocked his head. "But I guess I'm just not your type."

Rory floundered for words. "Wh-what?"

"I heard you," Dima said flatly. "I heard you loud and clear, Rory, when you said that just because I had a great ass didn't mean you'd ever want to date me."

Rory was drowning and he couldn't find air. He remembered that conversation. His heart banged painfully against his ribcage, hope and terror choking him.

"Army's a great guy," he finally managed. "But you really think I'm going to tell him just how head over heels I was for you? The whole team would have known about it five minutes later and I never would have lived it down. Dima—" He fumbled with the controls of the bed until he was sitting upright. "Dima, are you telling me you never—" He swallowed past the boulder in his throat. "*That's* why you never—that's why you said that?"

"I don't *know*," Dima snapped. "I still

don't remember that part, but I—" His breath hitched.

Rory held out a hand. "Dima."

"No," Dima said, glaring at him. "I'm so mad at you, Rory."

"I know," Rory repeated, still holding out a hand. "I know you are, baby. And I don't blame you. *Please* will you come here?"

Dima's glower redoubled but he took a step forward, then another. He sank into the chair and took Rory's hand.

Happiness was threatening to suffocate Rory. Dima's expression was still thunderous, but he was *there,* holding Rory's hand, and he'd just said—

"So just to recap," Rory said, stroking Dima's knuckles with a thumb, "you heard me say I wasn't into you because I was talking to the biggest gossip on the team and *trying* to keep my crush on you from being the source of relentless chirping from all sides. And you—" He took an unsteady breath. "You had a crush on me too, maybe?"

"No maybe," Dima snapped. "I *did.*"

"Which is why it hurt so much to hear me say I wasn't into you, so you got drunk and made sure I knew you weren't into me either."

Dima sighed. "Looks like."

Rory couldn't help the laugh, even

though it was soaked with tears. "God, Hank's right. We're both so stupid. Can I kiss you now?"

Dima bent and Rory met him halfway, stretching up into it, arms going around Dima's neck. For all the fury of a few minutes ago, Dima kissed as sweetly as he'd ever done, lips soft and tongue seeking entry as Rory opened for him.

It was several minutes before Rory could tear himself away.

"I love you," he said, and his heart was threatening to thump right out of his chest but he had to say it, Dima had to *hear* it. "I love you so much, Dima."

Dima folded forward and pressed their foreheads together, hands coming up to cradle Rory's throat. "I love you too, Rory." His voice was almost inaudible. "I'm sorry."

"Me too," Rory whispered. "But we're okay now, right?"

"Yeah," Dima murmured, and kissed him again, smiling against his mouth. "We're okay."

29

"COME ON, come on, we're gonna be late!" Rory was bouncing on his toes as Dima hunted for a tie.

"Relax," Dima said when he finally came up with a suitable one. "We have over an hour, what's got you so strung up about this?"

Rory hitched a shoulder, looking almost abashed. "Remember back before your memories came back, that day I, uh—did that thing?"

"Had a meltdown and basically demanded really aggressive sex from me without explaining why?" Dima finished. "Yeah, I've been meaning to ask about that. *Someone* keeps distracting me."

Rory gave him a brilliant smile, eyes crinkling, and Dima reeled him in for a kiss on general principles.

"Anyway," Rory said when they separated and Dima pointed him for the door. "Someone came to see me that day."

He told the story in fits and starts as they rode the elevator to the ground floor. There was shame in the way he hunched his shoulders and stared at the tiles, but Dima didn't interrupt. He let Rory tell it his way, until he got to the end.

"I was an asshole to him," Rory muttered, shoulders notching higher. "I was so fucked up about you, and I didn't know what to *do* and here's this kid wanting to come out *publicly*, like he has no idea the shitstorm in store for him—"

"His decision to make," Dima said gently as they headed for the parking garage.

"I know." Rory heaved a sigh. "Anyway, I told him real life sucked and it was gonna continue to suck, and he needed to just accept that, and then I kind of... ran away."

They reached the car and got inside, and Dima leaned across the gearshift, pulling Rory into a kiss.

Rory made a soft noise against Dima's mouth. "Don't," he said when they separate. "I don't deserve it."

"Yeah, I remember you saying that then, too." Dima squeezed his hand and started the car. "You said it yourself—you were fucked up. Not thinking right."

"I think I hurt him," Rory said. "And I can't fix that, or make it not have happened, but I can be there for him today. Because if he goes through with it, he's going to need friendly faces around him. And if he doesn't—"

"He'll still need the support," Dima agreed. "So this is why we flew home from Finland early, huh?"

Rory smiled at him, slow and sweet. "It's only June, we can go back after if you want."

"I don't care where we go, as long as I'm with you," Dima said honestly, and Rory made fake-gagging noises. "Shut the fuck up," Dima said through his laugh, punching him in the arm.

It had been three months since Rory's injury. With two of their star forwards out, the Otters had done their valiant best but it hadn't been enough to make the playoffs. As sorry as Dima had been for the season to end early, he was glad they'd had a chance to rest and heal. Rory turned out to be a terrible patient, complaining constantly when he was confined to the bed while his leg healed, but Dima could shut him up quickly with kisses, which almost always morphed into other activities.

They'd gone to Finland when the season ended, as soon as Rory was cleared to fly.

And now they were back, going to the draft to support a kid Dima had never even met. Dima took Rory's hand as he drove. Rory squeezed it but said nothing.

THE DRAFT WAS CHAOS—IT always was. Dima didn't miss it, or the barrage of questions and interest they got, appearing publicly together. But he and Rory were both professionals, and they answered every question they got with poise, until the first pick was gone. Rory patted Dima's knee and stood, surprising him, but just smiled at him when Dima sent him a questioning look.

He climbed the stage, no trace of a limp, and crossed it to shake Tony's hand, then Booth's. Then he turned to the microphone and gripped the podium as he said, "The Boston Otters are pleased to announce their choice, second overall, Jack Harman."

The cameras panned to where a slimly built young man was sitting. He looked faintly shell-shocked, maybe at the sight of Rory, but he stood and straightened his suit coat and descended the steps. He was going to pass right by Dima, and Dima stood on impulse, stepping out into the aisle. Jack stopped, eyes unsure, and Dima offered his hand.

When Jack took it, Dima pulled him into a hug. "We've got your back," he said into Jack's ear, and Jack stiffened. "Do what you need to do, we'll stand with you."

Jack clutched briefly at him, and his eyes were suspiciously bright when they separated. He said nothing, just smiled at him, and Dima stepped aside to let him continue his journey to the podium. He caught Rory's eye and a look passed between them. Dima smiled, soft and private, and Rory's mouth twitched up as he turned to greet Jack.

Dima settled back in his seat to watch. Maybe he hadn't expected his life to take this turn, but he sure as hell wasn't complaining. Whatever happened, he had Rory, and that was all that really mattered.

EPILOGUE

IT WAS a long time before Rory had a minute to himself, what with talking to the press, apologizing to Jack, and trying to get out of the building after everything. All told, he didn't have a chance to check his phone until he and Dima were in bed that night.

In the dim room, Rory opened his phone and scrolled through the notifications. One in particular caught his eye and he tapped on it.

It was from Carmine.

Proud of you, kid.

ACKNOWLEDGMENTS

This book was made possible by many long nights wondering why I do this to myself, heart-to-heart discussions with my friends about what exactly it is I find so irresistible about idiots to lovers, and my inner level of supportive readers.

First and foremost, Aaliya, platonic soulmate who just can't make herself care about hockey but for some reason does care about me enough to read my hockey books. You keep me writing.

Sarah, who makes my gorgeous covers and helps me untold amounts with formatting and publishing nitty-gritties.

CJ, who reads everything I write and is always willing to throw down in support of me for any reason whatsoever.

Kelly, who reacts in delighted all caps

anytime I tell her anything about whatever I'm writing at the time.

Yana, the best Russian fact-checker I could ask for and who graciously loaned me her name along with a ton of delightful insight on Russian diminutives. I promise I'll never call you Yanusya!

And everyone on Tumblr and Twitter who gives me feedback that they want more of my stories. I'm here because of you, and I'm so grateful for all of you.

ABOUT THE AUTHOR

Michaela Grey told stories to put herself to sleep since she was old enough to hold a conversation in her head. When she learned to write, she began putting those stories down on paper. She resides in the Texas Hill Country with her cats, and is perpetually on the hunt for peaceful writing time.

When she's not writing, she's watching hockey or blogging about writing and men on knife shoes chasing a frozen Oreo around the ice while trying to keep her cat off the keyboard.

Tumblr: greymichaela.tumblr.com
Twitter: @GreyMichaela
Facebook: www.facebook.com/Grey-Michaela
E-mail: greymichaela@gmail.com

Want to find out when her next book comes out? Sign up for her newsletter here or follow her on Amazon here

Keep reading for a sneak peek at Roughing!

BUTTERFLY

Felix was sitting in the back of the bar, out of sight of almost everyone and nursing a lukewarm beer when he saw them. The blond one was slim, similar to Felix's build but much shorter, and wrapped around his companion like a clinging vine.

His partner—Felix swallowed hard. His partner was *huge*. Easily six foot five, with dark hair that fell in soft curls into even darker eyes, and muscles to match his height.

And they were both looking at Felix.

Felix saluted them with his beer and an ironic tilt of his head. *Have fun*, it said. *Someone deserves to.*

He wasn't expecting the blond to disentangle himself and slide into the booth beside him. Up close, he had angelic features, hair so pale it was almost white, and piercing green eyes.

"Leo," he said. "I saw you looking at me."

"Who wouldn't?" Felix said, and took another swallow of beer. "You are easy on the eyes, *mon frere*."

Leo clutched his chest dramatically as the big man slipped into the booth on Felix's other side. "French!" he said, pretending to swoon. "I've always wanted to sleep with a French guy!"

"French *Canadian*," Felix corrected. He eyed the other man. "And you are?"

"Fisher," the man said. "And he's always wanted to sleep with a French Canadian as well."

"It's the accent," Leo sighed. He leaned on Felix's shoulder and batted white-blond lashes at him. "What's your name, gorgeous?"

Felix debated. Neither seemed like hockey fans, but the last one hadn't either, and he still bore the scars.

"Just call me French," he finally said.

"Less of a mouthful than French-Canadian, and I can think of other things I'd rather have in my mouth," Leo said.

Felix snorted. Fisher was so close his thigh was pressed up against Felix's, but instead of feeling crowded or stifled, Felix felt… safe. He looked up through his lashes into Fisher's dark eyes.

"Come here often?"

Leo squeezed closer, running a hand up Felix's bicep. "Not as often as we should, if you're what they have on offer," he said.

"So are you two a couple?" Felix asked.

Leo waggled a hand. "Ish."

"More like no," Fisher said. His voice was so deep it reverberated through Felix's bones. "But we play together sometimes."

Leo propped his chin on his hands. "Do you wanna play with us?"

"It is a tempting prospect," Felix admitted. "What would it entail?"

"You, me, him, and our dicks," Leo chirped. "Anything you want."

"Anything?" Felix swirled the beer in its mug. "That is a dangerous offer, *ami*."

"You don't look like the kind to hurt me," Leo said, shrugging. "And if you *did*, I've got Fisher. Trust me, he will fuck you *up* if you do something I don't want."

Felix arched an eyebrow at Fisher, who also shrugged.

"Someone's gotta look out for him," he drawled. "Since he was born without a self-preservation instinct."

"So?" Leo asked, a hand drifting across Felix's thigh. "You wanna or not?" Slim fingers traced the half-hard outline of Felix's dick, and he twitched.

"Condoms," he managed.

Leo rolled his eyes. "Duh. But first—" He cupped Felix's chin in one hand and leaned in, giving him time to pull away. His lips were soft and tasted like grape chapstick, and he moaned as Felix got a hand free and wrapped it around the back of his neck, pulling him closer.

Distantly, Felix heard Fisher swear softly, but most of his attention was on Leo, currently doing his best to climb into his lap despite the table in his way.

"My turn," Fisher rumbled, and caught Felix's chin, pulling his head around. Their mouths fit perfectly together, Fisher's breath hot and his tongue soft. Felix melted against him, making a helpless noise high in his throat, and Leo cupped his fully hard dick, rubbing it over the stretchy fabric of Felix's pants.

Felix couldn't figure out where to focus —the hand on his dick or Fisher's mouth, so hot and demanding. He tore free with an effort, gratified to see Fisher was breathing as hard as he was.

"Not here," he rasped.

"Aw, no exhibition kink?" Leo pouted.

"I have no wish to be recognized," Felix said, smoothing his hair back.

Leo's eyes widened. "Are you a celebrity? Wait, I know all the local actors and musicians and I don't know you, so who *are* you?"

"Doesn't matter," Fisher interrupted, and Felix glanced at him, grateful. "You know I'm not famous but I don't wanna be recognized either. So let's get out of here."

FELIX FOLLOWED them from the bar, shrugging into his coat against the chilly Portland night. He shouldn't have gone out, should have stayed home and focused on his game, watched tape of the Ravens for tomorrow night, done anything else, but instead here he was, halfway to drunk and about to have sex with two men he didn't know.

"We're calling a car," Fisher said when Felix caught up to him. "And we thought we'd go to my house—it's not far. Do you have anyone you can tell?"

"Yes," Felix said, pulling out his phone. "Sa—" He caught himself before he said Saint's name. "My friend Sinclair will want to know."

"Good," Fisher said. He rattled off the address and waited as Felix texted Saint, who was probably wearing sweatpants, curled up on the couch with Carmine and their dog.

He got an answer back almost immediately. *Play safe and hydrate. Don't stay out too late. Text when you get home.*

Felix glanced up. "How much longer until the car is here?"

"Two minutes, according to the app," Leo said. "We could have some fun while we wait?" He took a step toward him, eyes intent.

"No," Felix said instantly, stepping back, and was startled to see Fisher getting between them at the same time.

"Back of a dimly lit, smoky bar is a little different from making out on the public street," Fisher snapped. "You know that, Leo."

Leo sighed, holding up his hands in a gesture of surrender. "Can't really blame me for trying. I mean *look* at you two."

The car arrived then, saving them from further discussion, and Leo slid into the front seat as Fisher and Felix got in the back. Felix folded his long legs in, watching with amusement as Fisher tried unsuccessfully to do the same beside him.

"Fuck—Leo, scoot your seat forward."

Leo complied, and Fisher sighed in relief. His knees still pressed into the back of the seat and he had to hunch a little, his hair brushing the roof.

Felix stifled a snicker. "We should have gotten the luxury ride, I think."

"God, your accent," Leo sighed as the driver accelerated away from the curb. "Fish, you hear how he drops his H's?"

"Leo," Fisher said warningly, as Felix shifted his weight.

Fisher glanced at him, an apology in his eyes. Felix nodded, twisting his mouth ruefully. He could already tell Leo was going to be a handful. But worth it, he thought.

Sign up for Michaela's newsletter here to find out when Butterfly is available!

ALSO BY MICHAELA GREY

Beloved Scars Series
Broken Halo
Broken Rules
Broken Trust
Broken Promises

Hockey Romances
Blindside Hit
Odd-Man Rush
Roughing
Power Play

Standalones
Copper and Salt

9 781949 936254